James Hadley Chase and The Murder Room

>>> This title is part of The Murder Room, our series dedicated to making available out-of-print or hard-to-find titles by classic crime writers.

Crime fiction has always held up a mirror to society. The Victorians were fascinated by sensational murder and the emerging science of detection; now we are obsessed with the forensic detail of violent death. And no other genre has so captivated and enthralled readers.

Vast troves of classic crime writing have for a long time been unavailable to all but the most dedicated frequenters of second-hand bookshops. The advent of digital publishing means that we are now able to bring you the backlists of a huge range of titles by classic and contemporary crime writers, some of which have been out of print for decades.

From the genteel amateur private eyes of the Golden Age and the femmes fatales of pulp fiction, to the morally ambiguous hard-boiled detectives of mid twentieth-century America and their descendants who walk our twenty-first century streets, The Murder Room has it all. >>>

The Murder Room
Where Criminal Minds Meet

themurderroom.com

James Hadley Chase (1906–1985)

Born René Brabazon Raymond in London, the son of a British colonel in the Indian Army, James Hadley Chase was educated at King's School in Rochester, Kent, and left home at the age of 18. He initially worked in book sales until, inspired by the rise of gangster culture during the Depression and by reading James M. Cain's *The Postman Always Rings Twice*, he wrote his first novel, *No Orchids for Miss Blandish*. Despite the American setting of many of his novels, Chase (like Peter Cheyney, another hugely successful British noir writer) never lived there, writing with the aid of maps and a slang dictionary. He had phenomenal success with the novel, which continued unabated throughout his entire career, spanning 45 years and nearly 90 novels. His work was published in dozens of languages and over thirty titles were adapted for film. He served in the RAF during World War II, where he also edited the RAF Journal. In 1956 he moved to France with his wife and son; they later moved to Switzerland, where Chase lived until his death in 1985.

By James Hadley Chase
(published in The Murder Room)

You Must be Kidding

James Hadley Chase

An Orion book

Copyright © Hervey Raymond 1979

The right of James Hadley Chase to be identified as the author of this
work has been asserted in accordance with the Copyright, Designs and
Patents Act 1988.

This edition published by
The Orion Publishing Group Ltd
Orion House
5 Upper St Martin's Lane
London WC2H 9EA

An Hachette UK company
A CIP catalogue record for this book is available from the British Library

ISBN 978 1 4719 0400 4

www.orionbooks.co.uk

one

KEN BRANDON unlocked his front door and stepped into the lobby.

"Hi, honey! I'm home!" he bawled. "Where are you?"

"In the kitchen . . . where else?" his wife called. "You're early."

He made his way to the well equipped kitchen where his wife was preparing dinner. He paused in the doorway and regarded her.

The Brandons had been married for four years, and those years hadn't blunted Ken's feelings for her. Slim, blonde and more attractive than pretty, Betty Brandon was not only efficient in the home, but also efficient as Dr. Heintz's receptionist, and she had to be efficient since Dr. Heintz was Paradise City's top gynaecologist. She earned fifty dollars a week more than Ken did: something that secretly wrankled with him, but her earnings made it possible for them to live in a modest style which they both enjoyed, with two cars, a nice, bungalow in a good residential district and they were able to save for the future.

Ken was the head salesman with the Paradise Assurance Corporation. He earned a reasonable wage and trying to compete with his wife's earnings, he often worked out-of-office hours whereas Betty kept strict hours. She left home at 09.45 and returned at 18.00, her work day finished. This arrangement suited her as she could look after the bungalow

1

and prepare dinner for Ken, not always knowing at what time he would return. Betty prided herself on her cooking. With the aid of various cook books, every evening, she provided a good and tasty meal.

"Don't come near me, Ken!" she said sharply, seeing the light in his eyes and knowing from experience what he had in mind. "I'm cooking something important. You've arrived at the wrong time."

Ken grinned.

"Is there ever a wrong time? Honey, forget it! Two things: first, we are going to make certain our bedroom is still there, and second, I am going to buy you the best meal you have ever eaten. Let's go!"

Betty pushed him away.

"Now, Ken, stop it! The bedroom is still there, and will wait. We are not going out! I am cooking clam chowder, and let me tell you there is no restaurant anywhere that does a better clam chowder than I do! What's happened?"

"Clam chowder?" Ken moved to the saucepan and lifted the lid.

"Ken! Keep your hands off that!"

He hurriedly replaced the lid.

"Smells marvellous!"

"It is marvellous. What's happened?"

"Well, at least, let's have a drink." He went to the refrigerator and took from it a bottle of gin and a bottle of martini. "I have news!"

"Give me five minutes," Betty said.

He carried the bottles into the lounge, made two drinks, lit a cigarette and dropped into one of the comfortable lounging chairs. He waited impatiently.

Betty wasn't to be hurried. Ten minutes later, she came into the lounge. By then, Ken had already replenished his glass.

"So what's all the excitement about?" she asked, dropping into a chair by his side and accepting the drink he offered. "What's the news?"

2

"You may well ask." Ken grinned at her. He was now feeling slightly drunk. It was seldom he drank martini gins. "I've been promoted. Sternwood called me to his office this afternoon." He grimaced. "Frankly, honey, I nearly flipped. I thought I was going to get the gate. You know Sternwood. No one gets called to his office unless he is going to get the hot foot. Okay, so I went. Imagine! He has opened a branch office in Secomb, and he wants me to take charge. He says there is a big, untapped source of business there, and he expects me to get it. What could I say? No one argues with Sternwood. So I am now in charge of the new Secomb office."

"Secomb?" Betty stared. "But that's the black district."

"Not all black. It's the workers' district. There are lots of whites living there."

"What kind of insurance?"

Ken nodded approvingly. His wife was nobody's fool.

"A good question. Sternwood's idea is to go after the parents and sell them a safeguard policy for their kids. For a small premium, we can offer parents all kinds of coverage for their kids. In Secomb, there are around fifteen thousand possible prospects, and Sternwood is sure we will strike gold."

Betty thought.

"After dealing with all your rich clients, Ken, you won't like it, will you?"

"I've no choice. Anyway, it's a challenge."

"So you are in charge. How much more is he paying you?"

Ken grimaced.

"I'm still on my basic, but I get fifteen per cent on all business I bring in. Sternwood never gives money away. If he is right about the prospects—and I think he is—it could mean something substantial in commissions."

"How substantial?"

"I haven't had time to think about that. It depends on how hard I work."

Betty sighed.

"When do you begin?"

"The office is ready. I begin tomorrow." Ken finished his

drink. "There's one thing I don't dig, but I'm landed with it."

Betty regarded him.

"I would have thought there are lots of things you don't dig about this. What's the bad news?"

"Sternwood has a daughter. She is to work with me. According to him, she's a smart cookie, knows as much about insurance as I do . . . according to him. She is to handle the office while I do the leg work. It's not so hot to have Sternwood's daughter working with me. It'll mean I'll have to be on my toes all the time, not that I won't be on my toes all the time, but you know. . . ."

"What's she like, Ken?"

"No idea. I'll tell you when I meet her tomorrow."

"Let's eat."

While they were eating, Betty said, "I wonder if she's attractive."

Regarding her, Ken saw her worried frown.

"If she takes after her father, she must be something out of a freak show. What's bothering you, honey?"

Betty smiled.

"Just wondering."

"I'll tell you what's bothering me," Ken said. "I'll have a spy in the office . . . a hot line right to daddy's desk. I could be in trouble if she dislikes me or if I don't make a success of this job. I don't have to tell you that Sternwood is a sonofabitch. If his daughter puts in the poison, I'll be out of a job, and Sternwood could fix me for good. That's what's bothering me, honey."

"Darling . . . you know you will make a success of it." Betty put her hand on his. "Like it?"

"The best clam chowder I've ever eaten."

When they had finished the meal, Betty said, "What was that about checking to see if the bedroom is still there?"

Ken hurriedly shoved back his chair.

"How about the dishes?" he asked, getting to his feet.

"To hell with the dishes! Who cares?"

*   *   *

For a long period of time, Paradise City held the reputation as the billionaire's playground: the most expensive, lush-plush city in the world. Situated some twenty miles from Miami Beach, the City catered only for the very rich who demanded constant service. The army of those who supplied this service lived in Secomb, a mile drive out of the City.

Secomb was not unlike West Miami: a rash of walk-up apartments, battered bungalows, cheap eating places, tough bars where the conch fishermen drank and fought, and a major black population.

The new office of the Paradise Assurance Corporation was situated on Seaview Road which was in the heart of Secomb's busy shopping centre.

Having found parking with difficulty, Ken Brandon got out of his car and stood on the sidewalk to survey his new office. To Ken, it looked like a hockshop, but he had already accepted the depressing fact that he was no longer dealing with the rich and the plush. His possible clients would be struggling to make a living. They wouldn't think of entering an office that had the same luxury facade as the City's head office.

Aware that he was being watched by various black owners of nearby stores, he unlocked the door and entered.

He was confronted by a long counter. Behind the counter was a big room fitted with filing cabinets, a desk, a typewriter, a telephone: all looking second hand, which they were.

This room, he guessed, was where Sternwood's daughter would work. Lifting the flap of the counter, he walked across the room to a door with a frosted glass panel on which was printed in black letters: *Ken Brandon. Manager.*

He paused to study the glass panel. It gave him no pleasure. On the door panel of his office at headquarters, his name had been printed in gold.

He turned the door handle and walked into a small room equipped with a battered looking desk, a swivelled chair, a drab carpet, two upright chairs, facing the desk, a small window with a view of the noisy main street. On the desk was a telephone, a portable typewriter, an ashtray and a scratch pad.

He paused to survey his new kingdom and felt depressed.

He had been used to air conditioning in his headquarter's office. This small room was stuffy and hot. Crossing to the window, he threw it open and immediately the noise of voices and traffic poured in.

He had told Betty this promotion was a challenge. He grinned wryly. Some challenge! Sternwood had certainly handed him a change of scene!

He heard someone in the outer office, and he went to his office door. Standing in the entrance doorway was a tall girl, around twenty four years of age.

Ken regarded her with startled interest.

His first reaction was that this girl could be his first client. She had to be by the clothes she was wearing: a T shirt with a red heart where her heart would be and skin tight jeans, faded in the right places.

As he stared at her, he felt a stirring of his blood. This was some girl!

Her strawberry blonde hair, reaching to her shoulders, looked as if she washed it when she felt that way, but right now she hadn't, but the unkempt hair added to her sensuality. Her eyes were large and sea green, and the bone structure of her face was impressive: high cheek bones, a short, small nose and a wide full lipped mouth.

Still staring, Ken let his eyes shift to her body. Her breasts were like halved pineapples, straining against the T shirt. Her long legs, her leanness made her a superb, sensual young animal.

"Hi!" she said, and lifting the counter flap, she walked towards him. "You are Ken Brandon."

Good grief! Ken thought, this must be Sternwood's daughter!

"Right," he said. "You are Miss Sternwood?"

She nodded and smiled, revealing teeth that would be a rave to a toothpaste ad. executive.

"What a dump!"

She looked around, then walked over to the desk to examine the typewriter.

"Look at this goddamn antique!"

"Your father . . ." Ken began feebly, then paused.

"My father!" She snorted, sat down at the desk, picked up the telephone receiver and dialled. Ken watched her blankly, then when the connection was made, she said, "This is Miss Sternwood. Give me Mr. Sternwood." There was a pause, then she said, "Pop! I've just arrived. If you imagine I am going to work on this dead-beat, nail breaking typewriter, you must be out of your head! I want an I.B.M. electric, and pronto." She listened. Her face turned into stone. "Don't feed me that shit, Pop! I'm telling you: I either get it or I walk out!" She hung up.

Ken's eyes were goggling. The idea of anyone daring to talk to Jefferson Sternwood like that, even his daughter, shocked him.

"That takes care of that," she said. "What's your office like?"

"Fine . . . fine."

She got up, moved by him and surveyed his office.

"You can't work in a dump like this. It's like a goddamn oven!"

"It's okay. It's . . ."

She went back to her desk and dialled.

"Give me Mr. Sternwood," she said. Again there was a pause, then she said, "Pop! I am not working in this hell-hole without air conditioning. I want two portable conditioners here pronto. You . . . what?" Her voice rose a note. "Pop! You are talking through the back of your neck! If I don't get them, I'm quitting!" She hung up and winked at Ken. "We'll get them."

Ken drew in a long, slow breath.

"Mr. Sternwood must favour you, Miss Sternwood."

She laughed.

"Oh yes, I've handled him since I began to walk. He's all

7

wind and piss." She got to her feet. "Call me Karen."

He was aware she was studying him, and her searching gaze made him feel uncomfortable.

"You're not expecting to get business in Secomb dressed like that, are you?" she said.

Ken gaped at her, then looked down at himself. He was wearing a lightweight charcoal coloured suit, a conservative tie, a white shirt and highly polished shoes. When he had dressed that morning, he had surveyed himself in the long mirror in his bathroom and had decided he looked every inch the up-and-coming assurance executive.

"Like this?" he said blankly.

"You knock on a nigger's door, looking the way you do now, and he won't even open the door. Dress as I do. Look, suppose you go home and change into something casual? This is only a suggestion. You're the boss, but you won't get business in this god-awful dump looking like my Pop. Okay?"

Ken stared at her, thought, then realized she was talking sense. The lush-plush world of Paradise City was now behind him. He had to adapt himself to these new conditions.

"You've got something. I'll be back in an hour," and he left and drove home.

On the way, his mind was occupied with this girl. What a girl! The way she had talked to her father! Her looks and her body! Then he said, half aloud, "Watch it, Brandon! You are married to the nicest and best woman in the world! You've been married for four years, and you have never looked at another woman. Okay, Sternwood's daughter is sensational, so now's the time to really watch it!"

Betty had already gone to work when he returned to their bungalow. He went to the bedroom, dug out a pair of faded jeans, a sweat shirt and loafers from his closet and changed. It was his outfit when gardening. He regarded himself in the long mirror. More the Secomb image, he told himself, but his sleek haircut was a give-away. He ruffled his hair. That was the best he could do.

Getting into his car, he thought: "This girl's smart! I

should have thought of my image. Well, okay, I've—she's—fixed it. Now to work."

He didn't return to the office, but parked his car on Trueman street. On either side of this depressing street were broken down cabins, housing the black workers. He went from door to door, talking to black women about their children's future, and he got a surprise. Most of the women, after regarding him suspiciously, invited him in and listened. He realized as he talked that Sternwood had an idea: a great idea. The women showed immediate interest. Their kids meant more to them than anything else in the world.

"You come back tonight, mister. I'll talk to my husband."

Three women, obviously ruling the roost, signed up, and each gave him ten dollars to clinch the deal.

By lunch time, he had three sales and ten possible sales.

Feeling elated, he drove to the office, and as he entered a cool blast of air greeted him.

Karen was typing on an I.B.M. Executive and she paused to grin at him.

"I've got two sales," she said. "They just walked in. How did you make out?"

"Three and ten possibles. So you've got your typewriter and we've got air conditioning. You are a miracle worker!"

"Pop's the miracle worker if you know, as I do, how to handle him."

As he handed her the three contracts, he regarded her, again feeling a sex urge run through him. This hadn't happened to him when looking at other women since he had married Betty, and it disturbed him.

"Your father is smart," he said. "He has a great idea."

"Oh, he's smart all right." She studied the contracts, then laid them on her desk. "I'm starving. How about you?"

"I'll stick around. I don't think we should close the office lunch time. Someone might want to do business. Could I ask you to bring me a hot dog or something?"

"Sure. I won't be long," and she walked over to the counter, lifted the flap and crossed to the entrance door.

9

Ken watched her. There was this sensual movement of her hips, outlined by her tight jeans, that turned him on. When she had gone, the office seemed utterly empty.

Leaving his office door open, he sat at his desk. He stared into space for a few moments, then called Betty at Dr. Heintz's clinic.

"Can you talk?" he asked when she came on the line.

"Make it fast, honey," Betty said briskly. "How's it going?"

"Looks good, but there's the usual snag. I've ten prospects lined up for this evening. The trouble is the men are working and the wives can't sign. I'm going to be late. Don't expect me before ten."

"I'll have some cold cuts for you." Betty was always practical about food. "But it looks good?"

"Sure. Fine with you?"

"The usual." A pause, then she asked, "How about Sternwood's daughter?"

Ken was expecting her to ask that.

"Seems okay." He made his voice casual. "Early days. I'll give you details when I get home."

"Is she out of a freak show?"

Ken breathed heavily.

"Well, no. I had a surprise, but she is a real toughie like her father. She's definitely not my type."

Immediately he had said this, he cursed himself. After living with Betty for four years, knowing how shrewd and perceptive she was, he realized he couldn't have said anything more stupid.

"Oh? This is news to me, Ken. "Betty's voice turned frosty. "I didn't know you had a type."

"You are my type," he said hurriedly. "I just meant. . . ." What the hell had he meant?

"I must go. See you sometime tonight," and she hung up.

Ken blew out his cheeks, then stared into space. His thoughts turned to Karen Sternwood. He now wished he hadn't taken this promotion. At headquarters, his secretary,

10

who Betty knew and liked, was fat, middle aged and smart. He wished he had had the guts to have told Sternwood he would either remain as head salesman, working the rich, or he would quit. But how was he to know he was to be landed with a sexy piece like Karen? He knew instinctively that she was one of so many girls who had no scruples, sex-wise. If she got the urge to be screwed, she got screwed. He thought uneasily that she and he would now be in constant close contact: just the two of them, often alone in the office.

He ran a sweating hand through his hair.

It takes two, he told himself. Watch it, Brandon! Watch it!

Then forcing his mind away from Karen, he began to work on this idea that had dropped into his mind.

*　　　　　*　　　　　*

Ken returned home at 22.45, hot, thirsty, hungry, but triumphant. Out of ten prospects he had visited, he had landed eight sales, and the other prospects were eager enough, but wanted time to think. This meant that he had made $195 commission on his first day as branch manager, and he hadn't, as yet, scratched the surface. Yes, he thought, as he drove into his garage, Sternwood was smart.

While Karen had been lunching, he had drafted a prospectus, setting out in simple terms, what the Paradise Assurance Corporation could do for the young. Over the telephone, he had discussed his draft with the Sales Director at head office who had given him the green light. He had then hurriedly eaten the two hot dogs Karen had brought back with her, then telling her he would be out all the afternoon, he drove to the local school. He had talked to the Principal, a lean, youngish black who had welcomed his suggestions.

"This may be shooting at the moon," Ken said, "but it could jell. If it does, I couldn't cope at my office. Here's what I suggest: would you be willing to let me use the school hall one evening so I can talk to the kids' parents? Could I say I have your co-operation?"

The Principal didn't hesitate.

"Yes, Mr. Brandon. I'll gladly co-operate, but may I make a suggestion? If you want a reasonable turn out of parents, I assure you, knowing them as I do, an evening meeting would be disappointing. The fathers have been at work all day, and they won't be willing to go out again once they are home. The best time for a meeting would be Sunday afternoon at four o'clock. They will have had their Sunday dinner, rested and would then come."

Ken grimaced. That would mean giving up his own Sunday, but he realized the Principal was talking sense.

"Okay. I'll make it Sunday afternoon."

After more talk, the Principal gave him the names and addresses of four teenage blacks who he was sure, for a few dollars, would distribute the prospectus from house-to-house in the evenings, and could be relied on.

Ken then called on the local printers. They promised to have three thousand copies of the prospectus ready by Wednesday afternoon.

Satisfied, he had returned to the office. Sitting on Karen's desk, he had told her what he had done.

"How are you fixed for Sunday? I must have your help," he concluded. "Don't tell me you have a date."

"I had, but it doesn't matter. I think this is a marvellous idea. Pop will cheer." She smiled at him, and he was aware of the thrust of her breasts. "Anything else I can do? I do have a heavy date for tonight."

"Thanks a lot. This could jell, and I couldn't handle it without you," Ken said. "You get off. I'll be calling on these people. We've made a good beginning. See you tomorrow."

He watched her leave, and the slow roll of her hips as she crossed to the door again turned him on. Again the office seemed utterly empty when she had gone.

Now, back home, he walked into his living room. Betty was watching television, but snapped it off as he came in. She began to smile, then her smile froze.

"Ken! You haven't been working, dressed like that?"

12

"This is the new scene," he said, smiling at her. "Any beer? I'm starving!"

"It's all ready." She waved to the laid table. "I'll get beer."

He sat down and began to eat slices of beef and a mixed salad. Betty returned and placed a glass of beer on the table. She sat opposite him.

"Tell me."

While he ate, he gave her the details of his day. He didn't mention Karen, nor did he tell her he would be working on Sunday for that day was strictly reserved when they were always together. He decided he would keep that news to end his recital.

"I've made one hundred and ninety five dollars already in commission. How's that?"

"Marvellous! I knew you would be a success, darling." Betty paused, then went on, "But why this gear you're wearing?"

"When I got to the office—and what a dump!—I realized I was dressed all wrong," Ken said, helping himself to more salad. "Then Karen arrived, dressed any old way. So I came back and changed."

"Karen?"

"The Sternwood girl." Ken pushed back his chair. "That was just what I needed. Suppose we go to bed? It's getting late, and we've both got a hard day tomorrow."

"Tell me about her." Betty made no move to get up.

"I told you. She's like her father: tough and smart."

"What does she look like?"

Elaborately casual, he said, "The usual modern type you see on the streets. The usual uniform: skin tight jeans, T shirt, dirty hair, but she's smart all right."

He regarded his immaculately groomed wife: her hair, glossy, her make-up, even at this late hour, perfect, her simple blue dress more than pleasing, and he thought of Karen in her with-it gear, throwing sex off like a laser beam.

"Pretty?"

"She'll pass in a crowd." Now came the crunch. "There is

one thing I forgot to tell you, honey. This school meeting has to be at four o'clock this Sunday."

Betty stared at him, her eyes wide.

"This Sunday! Ken! What are you thinking about? It's Mary's wedding anniversary!"

At the back of his mind, Ken had known that something had been arranged for Sunday, but he had been so carried away with his idea of talking to a room full of potential prospects, he had dismissed whatever had been arranged for something that could be postponed.

He looked at Betty in dismay.

"I had completely forgotten! I'm sorry, but there was no way to get the school hall except this Sunday."

"But you can't do this to Mary!"

Mary was Betty's sister: a bossy, self opinionated elder sister who Ken thoroughly disliked. Her husband, a corporation lawyer, was in Ken's opinion, the biggest bore he had ever met. They had a large, imposing house in Fort Lauderdale. He remembered now they were to celebrate their tenth wedding anniversary. He remembered Betty and he had been invited to a Bar-B-Q lunch, then a big dinner with a firework display.

"The prospectus is being printed, honey. I'm terribly sorry."

Betty made a gesture of despair.

"Oh, Ken!"

"I just can't cancel, honey. Sunday is the only day. I'm terribly sorry."

"When will you be through?"

"Well, the meeting begins at four o'clock. It depends on the turn out. I should be through by seven."

Betty brightened.

"Then you could come for the fireworks."

Ken thought of listening to Mary's dreary yak and Jack's pomposity. Their friends were all drags, but he nodded.

"Sure. You'll go?"

"Go? Of course. The party won't be over until midnight.

14

You just must put in an appearance. Mary and Jack would be so hurt."

Ken restrained a sigh.

"Just as soon as this meeting is over, I'll be on my way."

She relaxed.

"I'll tell Mary and Jack why you have been kept. They'll be impressed that you are in charge." She got up and began to clear the dishes. As Ken helped her, she went on, "Will you be working from now on, so late?"

"I hope not. The trouble is, as I told you, the guy who has to sign is at work, but this meeting could fix it. If it is a success, then I don't see why I should have to work late. We'll have to see."

They went into the kitchen and cleared up.

"I suppose it's worth it," Betty said suddenly.

"What's worth what?"

"If you will have to work so late, Ken, I'm not going to see much of you."

He put his arm around her and gave her a little hug.

"Oh, come on, honey. Could be I won't have to work late. This is my big chance, and it's started well. I've already made a hundred and ninety five dollars."

"Money isn't everything."

"It helps, doesn't it?"

In bed together, Betty sleeping, Ken lay awake. The brilliant moonlight made patterns on the wall. No matter how he tried, he couldn't get Karen's provocative body out of his mind.

It wasn't until the sky turned pale, as dawn approached, that he drifted off into an uneasy sleep.

*   *   *

The school meeting was a flop.

Ken realized this the moment he entered the hall and saw there were only a few whites and blacks, sitting in the chairs that he, Karen and Henry Byrnes, the school Principal, helped by the four young blacks who had distributed the prospectuses, had set up: enough seats to accommodate five hundred people.

As he stood on the platform, surveying the people seated, he made a rapid count: thirty-four!

A flop of flops, he thought, but with a wide welcoming smile, he went into his carefully prepared sales talk. This took less than ten minutes, then he asked for questions. The questions came, and he answered them. There was a pause, then a white truck driver said it was a hot idea and he would sign. There was a flurry of voices, and by 16.30, twenty eight of Ken's audience had taken out insurance policies for the future of their kids. The remaining six said they wanted to think about it.

The meeting closed at 16.45.

When the last of the parents had gone, Byrnes came over to Ken.

"I'm afraid, Mr. Brandon, you are disappointed," he said, "but I can assure you, you have a big success. I know these people. They don't like meetings. That's why there was such a poor turn-out. For thirty-four of them to come here is an achievement. These thirty-four will be your salesmen. They are going to brag about what they have done for their kids. Here, in Secomb, people are all close neighbours. The word will go around. You wait . . . you are going to be busy."

Ken thanked Byrnes for his co-operation, shook hands and walked out into the hot sunshine with Karen at his side.

"I hope he's right," he said. "To me, that was a god-awful flop."

"I think he's smart," Karen said. "He could be right."

He regarded her. They both had agreed that they should present a better image for the meeting. She had on a simple green cotton dress. He wore a blue, light-weight jacket and grey slacks. He had only recently bought the jacket. It sported miniature golf balls as buttons which he thought made the jacket pretty sharp. As they stood in the hot sunshine, he thought Karen looked sensational.

The past five days had passed quickly. Twice Alec Hyams, the Sales Director, had looked in. Ken was secretly amused to see that Hyams was most obsequious when speaking to Karen, asking her if she was happy with her typewriter and the air conditioning. Karen treated him as if he were of no importance, and pointedly went on with her typing.

While waiting for Sunday, Ken had called on the various stores and shops up and down Seaview Road, introducing himself and talking fire and accident insurance. He didn't expect to get any business as everyone was already covered with other insurance companies, but he wanted to make contact and friends. His reception was good. Several of the store owners said it would be more convenient for them to take out policies with the Paradise when the present policies ran out, and would talk to him later.

Ken saw little of Karen who was kept busy card indexing, typing letters and talking to the various people who drifted in, making inquiries. In one way, Ken was relieved not to be in such close contact with her, but always, at the back of his mind, especially at night, he kept thinking of her, sexually.

The office closed Friday evening. He spent Saturday tending the garden, then he and Betty went to a movie in the evening and had dinner at a seafood restaurant. He kept wondering what Karen was doing. She had said she had to spend Saturday afternoon on her father's yacht. "That's a real drag. Pop's friends are creeps. Maybe I can find an excuse. . . ."

He had seen Betty off on Sunday morning. She had again urged him to come to Fort Lauderdale as soon as he could, and he had said he would.

Now, with the meeting over at 16.45, he realized with dismay, he could be at Fort Lauderdale within the hour. This meant he would be stuck with his dreary sister-in-law and brother-in-law until midnight!

Karen said suddenly, "Are you a handy-man around the house?"

Surprised, he stared at her.

17

"Why, sure. Why the question?"

"Just wondered. I guess you have a date right now. You couldn't spare a couple of hours?"

Ken's heart began to thump.

"I'm in no rush. I do have a date, but not until eight o'clock. Anything I can do?"

"I've just moved into my beach cabin. There are shelves to fix. Are you any good at fixing shelves?"

"The best shelf fixer in the business. Beach cabin? Do you have a beach cabin?"

"Strictly for week-ends. I was there last night after I got rid of Pop and his creeps. It's nice, but the shelves need fixing."

They looked at each other. Ken hesitated. A red light began to flash in his mind. He thought of Betty. He told himself to make some excuse and drive over to the gruesome party, but no excuse came to mind. Karen, looking at him, a provocative smile on her full lips, was blatantly offering herself.

"Maybe you want to go home," she said. "Some other time, huh?"

The red light snapped off and the green light came on.

"I'll be glad to help out," he said, aware his voice was husky. "How about tools? Maybe I had better go home and . . ."

"I have everything," she said. "No problem. Let's go."

They got in his car.

"It's a godawful drag," she said, as she settled herself beside him. "Last week, I got caught speeding for the third time, and the fuzz have taken my licence away for a month. Last night, I had to take a taxi to the cabin."

"The cops here are sharp," Ken said, as he set the car in motion. "Where do we go?"

"Paddler's Creek. Know it?"

Ken registered surprise.

"That's the hippy colony."

"Right. My cabin is about half a mile from them. When I get bored, I visit them. They visit me." She laughed. "I dig them."

"That's a pretty tough quarter."

"It's fine."

Ken stopped at the end of the lane and waited for a break in the Sunday traffic to move onto the highway. He kept telling himself he shouldn't be doing this. He should be heading for Fort Lauderdale, but when the break came, he turned left, away from Fort Lauderdale, and drove along the busy highway.

Very aware of Karen as she sat by his side, he found nothing to say. His heart was thumping, and his hands on the steering wheel were moist.

Karen seemed content to relax, humming under her breath, one long leg crossed over the other.

After a mile or so, she said, "Take the next turning on the left."

Ken slowed, signalled, and then, as other cars whizzed by him, he turned onto a narrow sandy road that led down to the sea. Ahead of him, he saw a thicket of Cypress and Mango trees.

"Park here," Karen said. "We walk the rest of the way. It's not far."

He parked in the shade of the trees, and they both got out. The evening sun was still hot. As he locked the car, Karen walked into the thicket, following a narrow, sandy path. He stood for a moment, watching the swing of her well rounded, provocative hips. Her walk really turned him on.

In the far distance, he could hear faint shouts, the sound of guitars and the thump of drums. The hippy colony was expressing itself. This part of the sandy beach was deserted. The citizens of Paradise City kept clear of Paddler's Creek. Following Karen for a longish walk through dense thickets and flowering shrubs, watching the movement of her body, his heart now slamming against his ribs, Ken threw all caution to the winds. He knew he was going to be unfaithful to Betty. As he walked after Karen, he tried to assure his conscience that most men were unfaithful to their wives. He told himself he loved Betty, and no other woman could replace her, but this

19

girl, walking ahead of him, had set him on fire. Betty would never know.

They came out of the thicket into a clearing. Ahead of them was a small pine wood cabin with a veranda.

"Here it is," Karen said. "All mine!"

He followed her up three steps and onto the veranda. Taking a key from her bag, she unlocked the door. Together, they moved into one big room, and she closed the door.

The air conditioner was on. The sun blinds were down and the room was dim and pleasantly cool.

He stood by her side, looking around.

Simply and comfortably furnished with a big settee and three lounging chairs, a T.V. set, a cocktail cabinet, an oval table with four upright chairs, and in the far corner, a king's sized divan, the room presented itself as a relaxing love nest.

His voice unsteady, Ken said, "Nice . . . well, to work. Where do you want your shelves?"

She laughed.

"Come on, Ken! You know as well as I do there are no shelves. I want you. You want me." She unzipped the back of her dress and let it drop around her feet. She had on only a pair of white panties. She held out her arms to him.

*   *   *

Ken woke with a guilty start, finding himself in darkness. For a moment or so, he didn't know where he was. He thought he was at home and in bed with Betty beside him. Then he remembered.

Darkness!

He groped around, found the bedside light switch and turned it on. By his side, satiated, Karen lay naked. Her long legs were spread wide, her hands covered her breasts. She opened her eyes as Ken swung his legs off the bed and stood up.

He was staring at his watch. The time was 20.20.

Karen had taken him like a widow spider, devouring him

and utterly draining him. In his wildest erotic dreams, he had never imagined a woman could do to him what Karen had done. His lust for her had completely evaporated. Staring at his watch, he could think now only that he would be suspiciously late to join Betty at the party.

"Look at the time!" he exclaimed. "I must go!"

"What's the panic?" Karen asked, her voice soft and lazy. "It was good, huh?"

He was struggling into his clothes.

He must have been out of his mind to have done this, he was thinking. Looking at Karen, as she lay on the bed, he felt revulsion. She was nothing better than a degraded whore. He had to get to Fort Lauderdale before the goddamn fireworks began!

"I've got to go! My wife is expecting me!"

She laughed, throwing back her head and arching her body.

"So you have to go. Don't get so worked up, Ken."

He was dressed now. He had no feeling except revulsion for her. He started to the door.

"Ken!" The cold snap in her voice stopped him. "You haven't said goodbye."

He paused, staring at her.

"I shouldn't have done it!" he said. "We were out of our heads!"

She slid off the bed and came to him. Her nakedness made no impact.

"Never have regrets, Ken," she said. "Always take an opportunity, and never regret."

He scarcely heard her. His one feverish thought was to get to Fort Lauderdale.

"I must go!"

"It's dark. Can you find your car?"

"I'll find it!"

"Wait!" She crossed the room and took a powerful flashlight from a drawer. "You'll need this." As she gave him the flashlight, her fingers caressed his hand. "You are a

21

marvellous lover."

He paid no attention. Snatching the flashlight from her, he left the cabin and ran towards the path that led through the thickets. His one thought now was to get to Fort Lauderdale.

Using the beam of the flashlight to light his way, he ran along the path. Halfway towards his car, surrounded by shrubs and trees, a stink of decomposition suddenly assailed his nostrils. He stopped, short, grimacing. Some animal had died, was his first thought. Moving forward slowly, keeping the beam of his flashlight playing on the path, he was aware the stink became stronger. It was now stomach turning.

He moved forward more slowly, then the beam of the flashlight lit up a body lying across the path. His heart hammering, bile in his mouth, Ken stared, then turned icy cold.

The body of the girl was naked. From her crotch to her rib cage, she had been ripped open. Her intestines lay in a gruesome grey puddle of blood by her side.

Ken shut his eyes, turned and started back along the path. Then the horror of what he had seen proved too much. He stopped and vomitted. For several moments, he stood motionless, sweat running off his face, then slowly, with lagging steps, he returned to the cabin.

He pushed open the door and moved into the big room. Karen had put on a wrap. She spun around as he came in. Seeing his deathly pallor, her eyes widened in alarm.

"What's happened?" The snap in her voice helped to bring him to his scattered senses.

"There's a girl out there . . . dead! Some maniac has murdered her!" He dropped into a lounging chair. "She's ripped! It's terrible!"

She stood over him.

"What the hell are you saying?"

"Can't you hear me?" he shouted. "There's a girl, murdered and ripped! We must call the police!"

Looking at his sweat covered face, his pallor and his shaking hands, Karen went to the cocktail cabinet and poured a huge Scotch. She thrust the glass at him. He drank greedily, shuddered and let the glass drop on the carpet. The jolt of the raw spirit stiffened him.

"Pull yourself together!" Karen snapped. "So there's a dead girl! It's nothing to do with you, and it's nothing to do with me! Who the hell cares? Get off to your wife!"

"I can't reach my car!" Ken said. "I couldn't go past that awful thing!"

"You can go by the beach. It takes a little longer." She went to her closet. Throwing off her wrap, she put on a swim suit. "I'll take you."

Ken looked at his watch. The time now was 20.45.

"It's too late! I can't get to Fort Lauderdale. . . ."

"Get hold of yourself! Call your wife. Tell her you have had a break-down. Then go home!" She snatched up the glass on the floor and poured another shot of Scotch. "Come on! Come on!"

He drank, then fortified, he took the telephone she thrust at him. For a moment he hesitated, then he dialled his brother-in-law's number. He leaned back in the chair, closing his eyes. There was a pause, then a booming voice said, "Hi, there!"

"Jack . . . this is Ken."

"Hi, fella!" Jack sounded drunk. "We're waiting for you. What's holding you?"

"Look, Jack, I've got a goddamn breakdown. I'm in a garage and the guy's working on it now."

"Hey! What's wrong?"

"God knows! The engine just died on me. I'm sorry, Jack."

"You can't do this to me, Ken! This is our anniversary! The big deal, Ken!" A pause, then he went on, "If everyone wasn't so stinking drunk, I'd get someone to collect you. Where are you?"

"On the highway. Look, Jack, as soon as it's fixed, I'll be with you. Maybe it won't take too long. Explain to Betty."

"Sure . . . sure. They're starting the fireworks. Come as soon as you can," and his brother-in-law hung up.

Ken replaced the receiver and stared up at Karen.

23

"That body. . . ." He shuddered. "We must call the police!"

"Ken! Use your head!" Karen exclaimed. "The police? They would want to know what you were doing here when you should have been at your party. Do you imagine anyone would believe you came out here to fix shelves? Do you realize what my goddamn father would do if he found out you and I had spent time in this cabin? He's dumb enough to think I'm still a virgin, but he's not that dumb to know once he knew we were together here, that we haven't been screwing! You would lose your job and I would lose this cabin! No police! Now, come on, let's go!"

The Scotch Ken had drunk was now hitting him. She was right, he told himself. No police! As she had said, this ghastly murder was nothing to do with either of them. Some other person would find the body. He realized that if Sternwood found out he had committed adultery with Karen, he would not only give him the gate, but he would be vindictive enough to get him black listed. He would never be able to get another job in insurance. Then there was Betty! God! What a mess he had got himself into!

"Come on!" Karen said impatiently.

He followed her out into the humid heat of the night. Half walking, half running, she led him down to the beach, then skirting the thicket—Ken couldn't bring himself to look at it, knowing the gruesome body lay there—she led him onto the beach. Then, once past the thicket, she moved inland. Turning a bend around a clump of scrub bushes, they suddenly came upon a man, walking fast towards them. The bright moonlight revealed him as tall, thin, bearded, wearing only a pair of tattered jeans, a duffle bag slung over his shoulder. His shoulder length hair and his vast beard only showed eyes and a long, thin nose.

The man stopped.

"Hi, there!" he said.

Ken had an uneasy feeling the man was staring at them.

"Hi!" Karen said, smiling.

Ken felt cold sweat break out over his body, but he forced a smile.

"Looking for Paddler's Creek," the man said. Ken guessed he was around twenty years of age.

"Straight ahead," Karen said. "About half a mile," and stepping around him, followed by Ken, she walked on.

"He'll know us again," Ken said huskily.

"That fink? He wouldn't know himself in a mirror," Karen said contemptuously.

Ken looked back. The bearded man was standing, looking after them. He raised his hand, then turning, headed towards the hippy colony.

"Keep on," Karen said stopping. "Just around those trees is your car." She moved up to him and her arms went around his neck. "It was good, huh?"

The feel of her hot arms made Ken flinch.

"It must never happen again," he said and moved away from her.

She laughed.

"They all say that. The reservoir fills up." Her fingers caressed his cheek, then turning, she ran across the sand towards the sea.

two

AT 20.30 quiet reigned in the Detectives' room at Paradise City police headquarters.

Detective 3rd Grade Max Jacoby was mouthing silently such phrases as: *Je voudrais un kilo de lait. Mais, mon petit, le lait ne se vend pas au poids: ca se mesure.*

Any hunkhead would know that, Jacoby thought, but desperately anxious to speak French, he mouthed the sentences from his Assimil *French Without Toil.* Jacoby's burning ambition was to take a vacation in Paris, and chat up the girls.

At his desk, across the big room, Detective 1st Grade Tom Lepski was wrestling with a cross-word puzzle.

Lepski, thin, tall, had been recently promoted. He was very alive to the fact that he was on his way up. His secret ambition was to become eventually Chief of Police.

The telephone bell rang on his desk. Scowling, Lepski snatched up the receiver.

"Detective Lepski!" he barked in his cop voice.

"You don't have to shout, Lepski," his wife said.

"Oh, you. Why honey, this is an unexpected pleasure," Lepski said, softening his voice.

"Where are my car keys?"

Lepski sighed and rolled his eyes to the ceiling. He loved his pretty, bossy wife, but there were times when he wished she didn't nag him so much.

"Car keys?" he said blankly. "I'm not with you, honey."

"You have taken my car keys! I have a date with Muriel

and the keys aren't here!''

Lepski sat up straight. This was fighting talk.

"Why the hell should I take your car keys?" he demanded.

"There is no need to swear at me! My car keys are not where I keep them. You have taken them!"

Lepski began to drum with his fingers on his desk.

"I've never seen your goddam car keys!"

"You should be ashamed of yourself, Lepski! Such language. My car keys are missing! You must have taken them!"

Lepski made a noise like a car back-firing.

"And don't make a noise like that to me!" Carroll snapped.

Lepski sucked in a long breath.

"Sorry," he said between his teeth. "I don't know a god . . . I don't know a thing about your car keys. Have you looked?"

"Have I looked?" Carroll's voice went up a notch.

Jacoby put aside his Assimil and settled himself to enjoy this. He had often heard Lepski and his wife shouting at each other on the telephone. As a performance, he had often thought, it was as good as any T.V. comedy act.

"That's what I said." Lepski was now on the offensive. "Have you looked under the cushions? In all your bags?

"Lepski!" The snap in Carroll's voice stopped him short. "My keys are not here! You have them!"

Lepski gave a laugh a hyena would have envied.

"Come on, honey! Why should I take your goddam car keys?"

"Stop swearing! You take things and lose them! You have them!"

Lepski shook his head sadly. There were times when Carroll jumped to stupid conclusions.

"Now, honey, you look again. You'll find them. Just act like a smart detective like me . . . really look."

He dipped his hand into his jacket pocket for his cigarette pack. His fingers touched metal and he gave a start, observed by Jacoby, as if he had been goosed with a hot iron.

"I've looked everywhere!" Carroll screamed.

Even Jacoby could hear what she had said.

Lepski fished his wife's car keys out of his pocket, stared at them, moaned softly and hurriedly put them back into his pocket.

"So, okay, honey," he said, oil in his voice. "You have mislaid your car keys . . . could happen to anyone. Now, here's what you do. Call a taxi. I'll pay. No problem. Take a taxi there and back. When I get home, I'll find the keys for you. How's that?"

"A taxi?"

"Sure . . . sure. I'll pay. Have a lovely evening."

"Lepski! I now know you have found them in your pocket!" and Carroll slammed down the receiver.

There was a long silence in the room. The drama over, Jacoby returned to his French studies. Lepski stared into space, wondering how, when he got home, he could find a hiding place for the keys that would convince Carroll she had unjustly blamed him.

Then the telephone bell rang on Jacoby's desk.

"Jacoby. Detective's desk," he said briskly.

A man's voice, low and husky, said, "I'm not repeating this, fuzz. Shake what brains you have alive, and listen."

"Who's this talking?" Jacoby said, stiffening.

"I said listen. You have a stiff to collect. Paddler's Creek. The first thicket on the drive down. A bad one." The line went dead.

Startled, Jacoby stared across the room at Lepski. He reported the conversation.

"Could be a hoaxer," he concluded.

Lepski, ever ambitious, snatched up the telephone and called the communications room.

"Harry! Who's covering Paddler's Creek district?"

"Car six. Steve and Joe."

"Tell them to investigate the first thicket on the drive down to Paddler's Creek, and pronto!"

"What are they supposed to find?"

"A stiff," Lepski said. "Could be a hoax, but get them

moving!''

He hung up, lit a cigarette, then got to his feet.

"Get your report written, Max," he said. "I'll wait for Steve to call back before alerting the Chief."

While Jacoby was hammering out the report on his typewriter, Lepski prowled around the room, giving a fair imitation of a bloodhound straining at the leash.

Twenty minutes later, his telephone bell rang.

"This is Steve. We have a real bad one here: a girl, ripped. Murder all right."

Lepski grimaced. It was a long time since there had been a murder in Paradise City.

"Stay with it, Steve. I'll get action."

At 21.15, four police cars converged on the thicket down to Paddler's Creek. Chief of Police Terrell, Sergeant Joe Beigler, Sergeant Fred Hess of Homicide, Lepski and three other detectives were the first to view the gruesome remains. Then Dr. Lowis, the police M.O. and two interns arrived with an ambulance. A police photographer unwillingly took ·photographs, then hurried into the thicket to vomit.

There was talk. Finally, the body was taken away.

Terrell went over to where Dr. Lowis was standing.

"What's it look like, Doc?" he asked.

"She was hit on the head, stripped and ripped. She hasn't been dead more than two hours. I'll tell you more when I get her on the table."

Terrell, a massively built man with greying hair and a determined jaw, grunted.

"Let's have it as fast as you can."

He walked back to where Hess, short and fat, was waiting.

"Okay, Fred, I'll leave you to handle it. I'll get back to headquarters. Find out who she is." Then signalling to Beigler, Terrell walked to his car.

Hess turned to Lepski.

"Take Dusty and chat up the hippies. Find out if she belonged there. Terry has polaroid photos of her. Get them from him."

Lepski went in search of Terry Down, the police photographer. He found him sitting on the sand, holding his head and moaning to himself.

Down, young, but a top class photographer, had only been with the Paradise City police for six months. With an unsteady hand, he gave Lepski three prints of the girl's face.

"Jee-sus! What a horrible . . . ugh!"

"You won't see much worse than that one," Lepski said. He studied the prints in the light of the moon. The girl wasn't pretty. Her face was thin, her mouth hard. A girl, Lepski decided, who knew all the answers, and had had a real tough life.

Dusty Lucas, Detective 3rd Grade, joined him. Dusty was around twenty four, massively built, with flat features of a boxer as he was: the best heavyweight of the police boxing team.

"Let's go, Dusty," Lepski said and got in his car. Dusty sat beside him. Lepski drove along the hard, white sand until he could see the camp fire and the gas flares, lighting the tents and cabins. He pulled up.

"We'll walk from here."

The sound of a guitar and drums were soft. A man was singing.

"Why the hell Mayor Hedley doesn't clear this scum out of the City beats me," Lepski growled. "Phew! What a stink!"

"I guess they have to live somewhere," Dusty said, reasonably. "Better for them to be here than in the City."

Lepski snorted. He walked briskly to where a group of around fifty young people were sitting on the sand, around a big camp fire. They were of any age from sixteen to twenty five. Most men were bearded, some with hair to their shoulders. The girls too followed a pattern: jeans, T shirts, hair mostly cut in a deep fringe, dirty.

The man, singing, was lean and tall. His face and head were so covered with thick curly hair it was hard to say if he was good looking or not. He spotted the two detectives as they came out of the shadows, and he abruptly stopped singing. He

30

was seated on an orange crate. As he got slowly to his feet, a hundred or so eyes regarded Lepski.

Somewhere in the darkness, a voice said, "Fuzz."

There was a long moment of silence and stillness, then the tall, lean man put down his guitar and walked around the seated hippies and paused before Lepski.

"I run this camp," he said. "Chet Miscolo. Something wrong?"

"Yeah," Lepski said. "Detective 1st Grade Lepski. Detective Lucas."

Miscolo nodded to Dusty who nodded back.

"What's the trouble?"

Lepski handed him the three polaroid prints.

"Know her?"

Miscolo moved to a gas flare, regarded the prints, then looked at Lepski.

"Sure, Janie Bandler. Looks like she's dead."

A sigh went through the group who were now all standing.

"Yeah," Lepski said. "Murdered and ripped wide open."

Again a sigh went through the group.

Miscolo handed back the prints.

"She arrived last night," he said. "She told me she was only staying a few days: had a job waiting for her in Miami." He rubbed his hand across his mouth. "I'm sorry. She seemed okay to me." He spoke regretfully, and Lepski, watching him, decided he was sorry.

"Let's have all you know about her, Chet." Aware of the tension in the group, Lepski sat on the sand. Dusty followed his example, sitting close to the gas flare, taking out his notebook.

This was a good move. The group hesitated, then they all sat down.

The smell of frying sausages and body dirt was a little overpowering to both detectives.

"Want a sausage, Fuzz?" Miscolo asked, dropping on the sand by Lepski's side. "We are all ready to eat."

"Sure," Lepski said, "and don't call me fuzz . . . call me

Lepski . . . right?"

A fat girl forked two sausages from the pan on the fire, wrapped them in paper and handed them to Lepski.

"None for this fuzz," Lepski said, not wanting Dusty's notebook to get greasy. "He's getting too fat."

There was a faint laugh around the group and the tension eased. Dusty made a comic grimace.

Lepski bit into his sausage and munched.

"Good. You folks know how to eat."

"We get by," Miscolo said. "Who killed her?"

Lepski finished the sausage. He told himself he must talk to Carroll about cooking sausages. Carroll was a non-expert cook, but a tryer. She constantly produced elaborate dishes that were always disasters.

"That's what we want to know," Lepski said. "She came here last night and said she had a job waiting for her in Miami . . . right?"

"That's what I said."

"Did she say what job?"

" Not to me." Miscolo looked around the group. "Did she say anything to any of you?"

The fat girl who had given Lepski the sausages, said, "We share a cabin. She said she had a job, working for the Yacht Club, Miami. I didn't believe her. From her style, I guess she was a hooker."

Lepski thought this was more than possible.

"What's your name?"

"Katey White."

"Katey is permanent," Miscolo said. "She handles the cooking."

That, to Lepski, explained why the girl was so fat.

"Did she have anything with her?"

"She had a rucksack. It's in the cabin."

"I'll want that." Lepski paused, then went on. "What happened tonight?"

"She said she was going for a walk," Katey told him. "I didn't like her. So she went for a walk, and I couldn't care less."

"Why didn't you like her?"

"She was too tough. I tried to talk to her, but her mouth was foul."

"When did she go for this walk?"

"Around seven."

"Any of you others see her?"

There was a chorus of "no".

"So she went for a walk, ran into trouble, got knocked on the head and had her bowels in a heap."

There was a long pause of shocked silence.

"Listen, you people, there could be a ripper around," Lepski said, his voice quiet and serious. "I'm warning you. Right now don't go for walks alone at night."

Again a long silence, then Lepski asked, "Would any of you know someone who would do a thing like this? Anyone kinky?"

"No one here," Miscolo said firmly. "We are one big family. No kinks."

Lepski thought, then asked, "Have you had any new arrivals? I mean someone who has arrived here within the past four hours?"

"A guy did drift in a couple of hours ago," Miscolo said. "Calls himself Lu Boone. He had some money and has rented a cabin to himself. I don't know anything about him."

"Where's he now?"

"Sleeping. He said he had thumbed from Jacksonville."

"I'll talk to him." Lepski finished the remaining sausage, then got to his feet. "Where do I find him?"

Miscolo also got to his feet.

"I'll take you." As they walked across the sand to the ten tiny wooden cabins, with Dusty walking with them, Miscolo said, "I don't want trouble here, Mr. Lepski. I've run this camp now for two years. There's been no problems. Mayor Hedley accepts us."

"Yeah, but don't kid yourself, Chet, you do have trouble."

Miscolo paused and pointed to the far cabin in the row.

"He's in there. You want me to stay around?"

"Suppose you go and wake him up?" Lepski said. "Tell him we want to talk to him. Then when you've got him awake, we'll move in . . . how's that?"

"You cops don't take chances, do you?" Miscolo grinned. "I'll leave him to you. I haven't finished my supper," and moving around Lepski, he walked back to the camp fire.

Lepski gave Dusty a wry grin.

"It was worth a try."

"That guy isn't stupid."

Lepski took out his .38 police special, sighed, then walked to the cabin and pushed open the door. Dusty, following training, dropped on one knee, his gun covering Lepski.

Lepski looked into total darkness. A rank smell of body dirt came to him. Then a light snapped on. Lepski moved sideways, his gun pointing.

A bearded young man, naked, sat up on the camp bed.

"Don't move," Lepski barked in his cop voice. "Police!"

The bearded young man flicked the dirty sheet across his lap, then stared at Lepski as he moved into the cabin.

"What do you want with me?"

Dusty came in and moved against the wall. He shoved his gun back into its holster.

Satisfied this hippy wasn't armed, Lepski lowered his gun.

"Checking," he said. "What's your name?"

"Lu Boone. Can't you fuzz let a guy sleep?"

Lepski sat down on the only chair. He holstered his gun.

"You've just arrived, Lu? Right?"

"If you want it spelt out," Boone said. "I booked into this cabin at five after nine."

"How did you come?"

"For God's sake! On my goddamn feet!"

"I mean which way?"

"Along the beach. I got a hitch to the top of the road and walked down, along the beach."

"This is a murder investigation," Lepski said quietly. "Did you see anyone? Hear anything? There's a girl's body in the first thicket along the road. You didn't go that way?"

Boone stiffened.

"You're goddamn right, I didn't! I don't know anything about murder!"

"The girl was killed around the time you were walking down the road. See anyone? Hear anything?"

Boone scratched at his beard and his eyes shifted.

"I didn't see anyone nor hear a thing."

Lepski felt instinctively he was lying.

"Look, Lu, think again. Did you see anyone on the road or on the beach?"

"I don't have to think again. The answer's no!"

"This girl was ripped wide open. The killer must have got blood on his clothes," Lepski said. "I want to look at your clothes."

"That's something you don't do, fuzz. I know my rights. Get a search warrant!"

Lepski looked at Dusty.

"Search this dump," he said.

As Dusty went over to the small closet, Boone jumped off the bed, stark naked, then stopped short as Lepski showed him his gun.

"Take it easy, Lu," Lepski said in his cop voice.

Boone sat down on the bed.

"I'll fix you, fuzz. I know my rights."

It took Dusty only a few minutes to go through Boone's clothes. He grimaced at Lepski.

"He's clean."

"I'll put in a complaint tomorrow!" Boone said. "I'll fix you, you goddamn flatfoot!"

Lepski gave him his wolfish smile.

"How would you like to be taken in as a pusher, Lu?" He took from his pocket a small packet. "I can always say I found this in your gear. Like the idea?"

Boone stared at the packet, then shrugged.

"Okay. Forget it. I'm losing my touch. Fuzz can't lose."

"You can say that again. Now, let's hear about you, what

you do, where you're from, when you're leaving here."

Boone again shrugged and began to talk.

Dusty wrote busily in his notebook.

*　　　　　　*　　　　　　*

Ken Brandon arrived back at his home at 21.30. During the drive, his mind had been active. What a godawful mess he had got himself into! Before long, the body would be found, then the police would move in. If it hadn't been for this gruesome murder, he would have driven to Fort Lauderdale and spent the rest of the night, celebrating Mary and Jack's goddamn anniversary. But the sight of the ripped body had completely unnerved him. Even now as he turned into the long road, leading to his bungalow, his stomach heaved.

This was Sunday night. Most of his neighbours would be out. He turned off his headlights and using only parking lights, drove slowly down the road. So he could establish an alibi for Betty and the police, he knew it was important to get home without being seen.

He drove to his garage door, flicked the gimmick to open the door and drove in. For a long moment, he sat in the car, thinking. Then leaving the car, he opened the door that led to the lobby and walked into the darkness of the living room. He crossed to the window and peered into the street. The three villas opposite were in darkness. He drew the heavy curtains, then groped his way across the room and turned on the lights.

So far, so good! he thought. He felt confident that he had arrived without being seen.

He made himself a Scotch and soda, then sat down. His thoughts darted like frightened mice. First, he had to convince Betty. He forced his mind to concentrate. After a while, he decided he must be truthful to a point. Betty was no fool. He planned his story, then satisfied, he thought of Karen.

God! That had been a mad, reckless mistake! He flinched at the thought that tomorrow he would see her again in the office. Sexually drained, Karen, to him, right at this moment, was a menace to his marriage and to his career.

Then he thought of the bearded man they had encountered. If the police got onto him, and if he told them he had seen Karen and himself, then . . . !

He wiped the sweat off his face.

He was still sitting in the lounging chair when he heard Betty's car. He drew in a deep breath and stood up.

A few moments later Betty came in.

"What happened, Ken?"

He seldom saw Betty angry, but he saw the signs now.

"I told Jack. I had a breakdown," he said quietly. "Was the party a success?"

"Ken! Why didn't you come? Everyone was asking. Mary was terribly upset!"

"There was something wrong with the ignition. I'm sorry, honey. I was delayed more than an hour."

"But you could have come!"

"Oh, sure. I could have come, but after the flop at the school house, after fiddling with the car, I just wasn't in the mood. I'm sorry, but that's how it was."

"A flop?" Betty looked concerned.

"You can say that again. After all the trouble I took, setting up five hundred chairs, I only got thirty-four people! Then when I got in the car, it wouldn't start. There I was stuck! Hell! I was ready to flip my lid. I took out all the plugs and got in a mess. I just wasn't in a party mood after all that."

"Didn't you do any business?"

"I got some of them to sign up, but what a flop! I came right back here to lick my wounds."

Betty went to him and put her arms around him. He ruffled her hair, feeling sure he had crossed the first hurdle.

"Darling, I am so sorry. I thought it was going to be so good for you," she said.

"You understand? I'm sorry too. I know I should have come, but I got so goddam depressed, I couldn't face a party."

She moved away from him and gave him that lovely smile he so cherished.

37

"Let's go to bed. I'll talk to Mary tomorrow."

While they were undressing, Betty asked, "What happened to Miss Sternwood?"

Ken felt a tightening in his stomach.

"She had a date. She went off before I tried to start the car," he said.

Betty went into the bathroom for a shower. Ken got into bed and lay on his back, staring up at the dimly lighted ceiling.

It's going to work out, he told himself. His groin still ached from the beating he had had from Karen. He was now relaxing. Then Betty slid into bed and turned off the light. Her arms went around him and she moved close to him.

"I'm turned on, darling," she said softly.

For the first time since they had been married, Ken failed her.

The following morning, Ken left Betty still sleeping, made himself a hasty cup of coffee, then drove to the office. Meeting Karen again was something he dreaded.

He unlocked the office door and went into his office, turning on both the air conditioners. He was working on the contracts he had made with the parents from the school meeting when Karen arrived.

"Hi!" she said, pausing in his office doorway and she smiled. "No problems?"

"No."

He looked at her. There she was in her skin tight jeans, her sweat shirt that emphasized her provocative breasts, her eyes alight, but he got no buzz from her.

"You look pale, Ken," she said. "We had a ball, didn't we?"

He pushed thirteen contracts across his desk towards her.

"Would you record these, please? I'll have the others ready in a while."

She laughed.

"Sure." She came over and picked up the contracts. "Strictly business this morning, huh?"

He didn't look up, but frowned down at the contract lying before him.

"Oh-ho!" Again she laughed. "Mister guilty conscience. You'll recover," and she walked back to her office, swinging her hips.

Ken sat back. He must get rid of her, he told himself. This situation just couldn't continue. But how? He sat staring into space, listening to the busy clack of Karen's typewriter. How to find some acceptable excuse to persuade Sternwood to move his daughter to head office.

Then the prediction of Henry Byrnes, the school's principal, became a fact.

A sudden murmur of voices in the outer office brought Ken to his feet. He found more than a dozen black people standing before the counter. They all wanted to know what the Paradise Assurance Corporation could do for their children.

From then on, Ken and Karen were busy. The morning passed swiftly. Both of them had sandwich lunches sent in from the Snack bar across the street. It wasn't until 16.00 that they had time to relax.

"Phew! This has been quite a day," Karen said. "Pop will be pleased."

"So it wasn't such a flop. I'll call Hyams. This is something to boast about."

Ken went to his office and checked the number of policies he had issued, then, as he was reaching for the telephone, he heard the outer door open. Yet another client, he thought, and getting to his feet, he looked into the outer office.

A tall, thin man with hard blue eyes was standing at the counter. Ken felt a rush of cold blood down his spine. Police! He immediately recognized Detective Tom Lepski from police headquarters. Although Ken had never spoken to this man, he had often seen him either driving or walking around the City. One of Ken's golfing friends had said, "You see that guy? He'll be Chief of Police when Terrell retires: real smart."

Ken moved back out of sight. He took out his handkerchief to mop off the rush of cold sweat. His mind flashed to the bearded hippy. He must have given the police a description of both Karen and himself!

Lepski leaned on the counter and regarded Karen with approving eyes. Lepski was susceptible to any girl who he regarded as a sexy piece.

Karen stopped typing, got up and swished her way across the room to the counter. The sway of her breasts, the swing of her hips were not lost on Lepski who gave her a leering smile.

"Miss Sternwood?"

Karen also knew this man was a detective. Seeing his smile, she returned it with an up and under flutter of her eyelashes which intrigued Lepski.

"Well, if it isn't," she said, "someone is wearing my clothes."

Lepski gave his soft wolf laugh.

"You are a police officer," Karen went on. "Have you children, Mr. Lepski?"

Thrown off his stride, Lepski gaped at her.

"Children? Why, no. I . . ."

"You must be married," Karen said. "A beautiful hunk of manhood like you just couldn't be single."

Lepski made a noise like a cat fed sardines.

"Miss Sternwood . . ."

"So you are thinking of raising a family and you want insurance coverage," Karen went on, thrusting her breasts at him. "Mr. Lepski, you have come to the right place. To insure unborn children will give you a very low premium."

Lepski got hold of himself. The very idea of having children, plus Carroll to contend with was his idea of a horror nightmare.

He was well aware that Karen was the daughter of one of the richest and most influential men in the City. The Homicide squad, searching around the murder scene, had come upon Karen's cabin which was within two hundred yards of where the body was found. Hess, who knew everything there was to know about the rich in the City, had told his men not to approach the cabin. He had reported to

Terrell who had told Lepski to talk to Karen who would be at the Secomb branch of the Assurance Corporation.

"Handle her with kid gloves, Tom," Terrell warned. "We don't want to get Sternwood sour. My information is that she is a top class bitch."

"Miss Sternwood," Lepski said firmly, "I am investigating a murder."

Karen's eyes opened innocently wide.

"Is that right? So you are not planning to raise a family just yet?" She gave him a sexy smile. "Maybe later."

Lepski eased his shirt collar with a hooked finger.

"Last night, Miss Sternwood, a girl was murdered within a couple of hundred yards from your cabin. Were you in the cabin last night?"

"Yes, I was, alone, I like being alone sometimes. I like to unwind after working in this dump all the week." Karen fluttered her eyelashes at him. "Don't you like to be alone sometimes, Mr. Lepski?"

Into Lepski's shrewd mind came a doubt. This sexy piece might be trying to con him.

"You heard nothing? No screams? Nothing?"

"I was watching T.V. Do you dig T.V.? I guess you're too busy to be able to watch much. I find it relaxing."

Lepski smiled his wolfish smile.

" What were you watching, Miss Sternwood?"

He saw her eyes flicker, and he knew, from his long experience as a cop, he had sunk in a punch that told him she was lying.

"Oh, something." She shrugged, once more on even keel. "Does it matter? Some goon screaming."

"You didn't hear a car?"

"I've told you, Mr. Lepski, I didn't hear a thing. Who is this girl? What happened?"

Lepski stared at her, his cop eyes cold.

"It was a messy murder, Miss Sternwood. I'm glad you were safe in your cabin, watching T.V. I wouldn't like anyone to see what this killer did to this girl."

41

Karen grimaced.

"How awful!"

"That's right, Miss Sternwood. So you can't help me? You saw no one, heard nothing . . . right?"

She tilted her chin at him.

"That's right."

They regarded each other, then Lepski tipped his hat.

"Thanks, Miss Sternwood." He paused, then gave her a long hard cop stare. "Miss Sternwood, this is no business of mine, but spending weekends in that lonely cabin entirely on your own could be dangerous."

"Thank you, Mr. Lepski." She smiled brightly at him. "As you say, no business of yours."

As soon as Lepski had gone, Ken appeared, white faced and shaken.

Looking at him, Karen said sharply, "Come on! Relax!"

"That guy with the beard we ran into!" Ken said. "If the police find him and he talks, he could prove you were lying."

Karen returned to her desk and sat down.

"It would be his word against mine, and my word, plus Pop's word, draws a lot of water," she said and began typing.

*   *   *

At 17.00, there was a conference around Chief of Police Terrell's big desk. Sitting before him were Sergeant Beigler, Sergeant Hess, Detective 1st Grade Lepski and Detective 3rd Grade Jacoby.

The various police reports that had flowed onto Terrell's desk had been summarized: reports from Hess, the M.O., Lepski, Jacoby and other detectives.

"Janie Bandler," Terrell said. "She kept a diary. She has been on the hoof as an itinerant prostitute for some years. That's about all we know of her. Dr. Lewis tells us she was knocked on the head, stripped, raped, strangled and ripped. This is a savage, sex nut murder. So far, none of the hippies have come forward with any useful information. None of them seemed to have seen or heard anything."

"I'm checking everyone of them out," Hess said. "There are some fifty of them at the time of the killing. It'll take a little time."

Terrell nodded.

"From what we have, it would seem the only possible lead is Lu Boone who admits being near the scene of the killing at the time of the killing. The killer must have had blood on his clothes." Terrell glanced at Lepski. "You checked his clothes and found them clean."

"Yeah, but I'm pretty sure he knows something. He either saw someone or else he's the killer. When I questioned him, I got the impression he was lying. He played it too cool. He says he has money, likes to live rough and plans to stay at the colony for a couple of weeks."

"Check on him, Fred," Terrell said.

"I'm doing it," Hess returned.

"Right. Now we come to Miss Sternwood who owns this cabin within two hundred yards of the murder scene."

"I talked to her," Lepski said. "She's a smart sexy cookie. She admits being in the cabin at the time of the murder, watching T.V. She claims to have been listening to some goon singing. I've checked all the channels, but at that time no one was singing. My guess is she had some guy there and was screwing. A piece like her just wouldn't spend the week-end alone, watching T.V."

"That's not our business," Terrell said. "She's Sternwood's daughter . . . remember that. We'll forget her." He turned to Jacoby, "What impression did you get of this man who 'phoned the squeal?"

Jacoby shrugged.

"Husky voice; could be any age; anti-police. No hope of tracing the call. It didn't last more than five seconds."

"It could have been the killer," Terrell said. He looked around at the men sitting before him. "This could happen again. This is a sex nut and he could be on the prowl. We've got to find him, and fast." To Hess, "If you want more men,

Fred, I'll borrow some from Miami."

The telephone bell rang. It was a call for Hess. The others waited while Hess talked to one of his men who had been, with others, searching the thickets and the sand around the murder scene.

"Let's have it right away," he said and hung up. To Terrel, he said, "Jack has found an odd jacket button: a miniature golf ball, half buried in the sand and about three yards from the body. Could be our first clue."

*　　　　　*　　　　　*

Fat Katey White was cooking sausages over the camp fire when Lu Boone joined her. She was on her own. It was her pride that there was always a constant supply of sausages ready for anyone who felt hungry. Sausages and spaghetti were the staple diet of the colony. The rest of the colony were either swimming or earning a few dollars wherever a dollar could be earned.

Accepting a sausage, Lu squatted by her side.

They got talking. Katey thought Lu was a super man. She loved his beard, his muscles and his jeering green eyes. Lu had a talent for turning girls on. This was about his only talent as his father, a staid Houston judge, had sadly discovered. Lu was a law drop out. He considered his father and his mother were the world's biggest drags. He had left home when he was seventeen years of age, and since then, now twenty-three, he had bummed around, picking up some kind of living, doing any job from dish washing to garage work, but happy to be free from the suffocating atmosphere of his home. But after six years of living rough, he had come to the conclusion that money, after all, was important. He had begun to dream of being rich: not peanuts, but real money, and he had also come to the conclusion that he just wasn't going to become rich by settling to some dreary nine-to-five.

Arriving at Jacksonville three days ago, he found he hadn't enough money to buy himself even a hot-dog. His hunger over-came the last of his scruples. Walking aimlessly through Confederate Park, he came upon a well dressed, old woman, sitting on a bench, sound asleep. By her side was a large lizard-skin handbag. It was the work of a moment to whip up the bag and run swiftly into the flowering shrubs. The net yield of the bag was an unbelievable $400.

Katey had been living in the colony now for two years, and what she didn't know about the City, most of the people and their way of life, could be written on the head of a pin.

Seeming to be chatting idly, Lu got from her that Karen Sternwood, the daughter of one of the richest men in the City, owned the cabin right where this hooker was murdered.

"Karen is okay," Katey said. "She comes here from time to time. In spite of all her money, she's our people. Chet digs her."

Lu became alert.

"If she's that rich, what's she doing living in a shack like that?" he asked, reaching for another sausage.

"It's her love nest," Katey explained. "Her old man is a real drag. A girl needs to get screwed now and then. If her old man ever knew what went on in that cabin, he would flip his stupid lid."

"Would she care?"

Katey laughed.

"Sure she would. Right now she has everything. She once told me if her old man found out, he'd cut her off without a dime." She looked longingly at the sausages she was cooking, but she checked the impulse to take one. She hated being known as Fat Katey. "But Karen likes work. Her old man started a branch office in Secomb. She works there: a nine to five stint that would drive me out of my tiny mind."

"Is she in charge there?" Lu asked, ever probing.

"Oh, no. Ken Brandon is in charge." Katey heaved a sigh. "There's a lovely man!"

"Why do you say that, Katey?"

"He's just like Gregory Peck, when young, and he's nice. He once gave me a hitch into the city." Katey closed her eyes

45

and sighed again. "He really turned me on."

Lu's mind shifted to the man who had been with Karen. Tall, dark, and maybe like Peck. It made sense. A guy working all day with a hot piece like Karen would want to screw her.

"No romance for you, Katey?" he said with a sympathetic smile. "I suppose he's married?"

"Oh, sure. His wife is real smart. She works for Dr. Heintz. He fixes all these rich creeps who get pregnant."

"Does Brandon get along with his wife?"

"Sure. They get along fine together. Any girl in her right mind would get along with him!"

Lu decided he had asked enough questions. He switched the subject and asked Katey how long she planned to stay with the colony.

Katey shrugged.

"I've got nowhere else to go. I guess I'll stay as long as I'm wanted."

Lu patted her fat hand.

"You'll always be wanted, chick. You've got that thing." Then he got to his feet. "I'll take a look around. See you, and take care."

Katey watched him walk towards his cabin.

You've got that thing!

She felt a pang. How she wished she had! Then the impulse to eat a sausage proved too much for her.

Back in his cabin, Lu sat on the camp bed. He opened the telephone book and found Ken Brandon lived on Lotus Street. He scribbled the address down on a scrap of paper. Then he counted his stolen money. He was worth $350. He lit a cigarette and sat for a long time, thinking.

This could be his big take, he told himself, but he would have to handle it carefully.

First, he must survey the scene. He must find out about how much Brandon was worth. There would be no problem with the Sternwood girl. According to Katey, her old man was loaded with the stuff. According to Katey, Brandon and his wife were close. This night out was probably Brandon's first slip up: a strong lever for getting money from him.

If he handled it right, Lu told himself, stubbing out his cigarette, he could pick up ten thousand dollars: the thought excited him.

Then he frowned. If he went ahead, this would be extortion. His year in law school had taught him this was a serious offence. Again he thought. He was already a thief. Extortion? If he played this smart, he wouldn't get caught. Ten thousand dollars!

He scratched his beard while he continued to think. Step by step, he finally told himself: survey the scene.

Getting to his feet, he went into the bathroom and trimmed his beard and hair closely. Then stripping off, he took a shower. Dressed in his best hip-huggers and a white shirt, he surveyed himself in the bathroom mirror. He was satisfied that he wouldn't attract the attention of some nosey fuzz. He looked almost respectable!

Leaving the cabin, he walked over the dunes to the highway. He waited for a City-Secomb bus, then was conveyed to Secomb. While sitting in the crowded bus, he decided he would have to become mobile. After wandering around the crowded streets of Secomb, he came upon a car mart. Two hours later, he drove away in a battered VW. He had paid $155 for the half-wreck, but not before he had squeezed from the dealer a new set of plugs. He was satisfied that the car would run for another five hundred miles. His garage experience had paid off.

He had asked the car dealer where to find the branch office of the Paradise Assurance Corporation. Following the car dealer's directions, he drove to Seaview Road, and was able to park within twenty yards of the Assurance office. The time now was 13.00. He hadn't been sitting in the car for more than ten minutes when he saw Ken Brandon leave the office and walk over to the quick-lunch bar, across the road.

Lu immediately recognized Brandon as the man he had seen with Karen on the beach.

Check! he thought.

He then drove into the City. He found parking and bought a map of the City from a drug store. Returning to the car, he located Lotus street. He drove there, then leaving the car at the top of the road, he walked down, passing bungalows and villas until he came to Brandon's bungalow. Slowing, but not stopping, he regarded the bungalow with its trim garden, and he nodded to himself. A guy who could afford a place like this, he thought, must be worth at least five thousand dollars.

Returning to his car, he drove back to Secomb, and again found parking near the Assurance office. For some minutes, he watched black people entering the office. He had to be sure that the girl who had been with Brandon was indeed Karen Sternwood. He hesitated. Would she recognize him if he walked into the office? He had trimmed his hair and beard. As she had only seen him in the moonlight, he decided it was unlikely she would recognize him. But suppose she did? Did it matter? He would have preferred the element of surprise, but it was worth the risk.

Leaving the car, he walked over to the office and entered.

Karen was talking to an anxious looking black man.

Lu paused in the doorway and looked hard at her. No doubt about it! She was the girl!

Karen glanced at the man who had come in and who was staring at her. She immediately recognized him. A little shock ran through her, but not for an instant did her expression betray her shock.

"A few minutes," she said with her sexy smile.

Watching her, Lu was convinced she hadn't recognized him. He smiled.

"Parking problems," he said. "I'll be right back," then he returned to his car.

Karen forced her mind to the problems of this worried black man who seemed so desperate to protect his brood of ten children. As she began again to explain the policy she was offering to take care of his children, she thought this man who had just come in, who had stared at her, and had now gone, meant real trouble.

48

A TALL grey-haired man walked into Police headquarters. Someone had once told him he looked like James Stewart, the movie actor, and from then on, he had aped the actor's mannerisms. He was Pete Hamilton, crime reporter on the City's T.V. network. As he covered scandal, society gossip as well as crime, he had a vast audience. He was regarded by the police as the original pain in the ass.

Ignoring Sergeant Tanner who was at the charge desk, he walked briskly down the corridor and swept into Beigler's tiny office.

"Hi, Joe!" he said, coming to rest before Beigler's desk. "Let's have it! I'm on the air in a couple of hours." He pulled up a chair, sat down and took out a notebook. "Janie Bandler. What clues? What are you guys doing?"

Beigler sighed. He would have liked to have caught hold of Hamilton and kicked him out of his office, but no one did that to a man of Hamilton's influence.

"It would seem," Beigler said carefully, "we have a sex nut around. Apart from rape, there seems no other motive. We are checking. I don't have to tell you, Pete, that finding a nut is the hardest nut to crack."

"You're becoming quite a wit, Joe. So, okay, what have you got so far? Any clues? Any leads? This poor girl . . . what do you know about her?"

"No clues so far," Beigler said. He never gave out information unless he had to. "Janie asked for trouble. She was a whore. Maybe she ran into some guy, propositioned him and was unlucky.

"He ripped her . . . right?"

"Sure."

Hamilton stared at him.

"A ripper could do it again."

"Yeah, but he could have been passing through the City. We don't want to start a panic, Pete, so play that angle down."

Hamilton's eyes narrowed.

"Listen, Joe, I have a sixteen year old daughter! Girls should be warned. If there is a nut around, it's Mayor Hedley's and your job to show the red light. I don't give a damn about panic! Girls must be warned!"

"I can't stop you," Beigler said quietly. "The Chief is talking now with the Mayor."

"Have you talked to Chet Miscolo?"

"We've talked to him."

"Didn't he come up with anything?"

"We have the names and addresses of all those in the colony last night," Beigler said. "We're checking each and everyone. It'll take a little time. Right now as I've said we have nothing to go on. As soon as we have, I'll alert you."

Instinct told Hamilton that Beigler was holding back on him.

"Do you want me to say the police don't know a thing?"

Beigler gave him a sour smile.

"You say what you like, Pete. It's early days." He waved to a mass of papers littering his desk. "We're checking. Just remember this girl was a whore and she asked for trouble. In spite of what she was, we will find her killer. That's our job. If you want to be helpful, say we are doing just that."

Hamilton got to his feet.

"Got a photo of her, Joe?"

Beigler produced a copy of the polaroid print. Hamilton studied it, and grimaced.

"Yeah, I see what you mean: a real toughie. Okay, I'll play it down. After all, as you say, she was only a hooker."

While this interview was in progress, Lepski with Jacoby was visiting the various men's wear shops in the City.

While Lepski was driving, Jacoby asked, "How did that car key drama with Carroll work out, Tom?"

Lepski grinned.

"Did I get away with that! I had the goddamn keys in my pocket. I thought they were mine! When I got home last night I put them under her car mat. I got her to apologize!" He pulled up outside Henry Levine's tailor shop. "When you get married, Max, you watch it! A husband has to act smart all the time or else he's in trouble."

They entered the shop and asked for Mr. Levine. This was the fifth unsuccessful call on tailors they had made.

Mr. Levine, fat and aging, but prosperous, immediately identified the golf ball button.

"Sure, Mr. Lepski," he said. "This is a speciality of mine." He walked to a rack and produced a blue jacket with golf ball buttons. "See? Nice idea, huh?"

"We are trying to trace this button, Mr. Levine. Can you tell us who has bought one of these jackets?"

"No problem. Just wait," and Levine went into his office. While waiting, Lepski examined the rack of jackets. He found one that attracted his attention.

"How about this, Max?" he asked. "Pretty sharp, huh?"

Jacoby examined the jacket of pale yellow with broad blue stripes. He thought it was an abortion.

He made a non-commital grunting noise. Lepski continued to regard the jacket, then taking off his own jacket, he slipped on the jacket and surveyed himself in the long mirror.

"Boy! Is this great?"

Jacoby thought Lepski looked like an escapee from a circus.

"You could stop the traffic in that," he said.

Lepski looked suspiciously at him.

"Don't you like it?"

"I don't have to live with it," Jacoby said, "but would Carroll like it?"

"Yeah." He again regarded himself, frowning. He realized

51

that Carroll would create a scene if he took the jacket home.

Levine came from his office.

"Ah, Mr. Lepski!" he exclaimed, seeing Lepski had put on the jacket. "I've always thought you had a touch of class. Now that jacket is something very, very special. It's an original. You won't find a similar jacket in the City. Feel the cloth . . . wonderful! Look at yourself! It is made for you! It gives you a look of considerable distinction."

Lepski hesitated, stroking the cloth. He again regarded himself in the mirror.

Seeing his hesitation, and because Jacoby was fond of both Lepski and Carroll, he said, "Carroll!"

Lepski sighed, removed the jacket and put on his own. Looking at himself in the mirror again, he decided he looked like any other cop, and he sighed again.

"Mrs. Lepski likes to be around when I choose clothes." He gave a false laugh. "She imagines her choice is better than mine."

Levine who had already encountered Carroll, abandoned the sale. He handed Lepski a slip of paper.

"Those are the names and addresses of my clients who bought the jacket: only four of them. Is something wrong, Mr. Lepski?"

"Just routine, and thanks," Lepski said, and he left followed by Jacoby.

Back in their car, Lepski examined the list.

"Ken Brandon!" he exclaimed. "This button places him on the murder scene!"

"Why say that?" Jacoby demanded. "We don't even know if he has a button missing on his jacket!"

"I bet he has!" Lepski got excited. "I bet he was with that sex chick last night in her cabin. Use your head. Brandon works all day in close contact with her. Ask yourself how you would react to be in daily contact with dynamite like her."

"If I were in Brandon's place, knowing she was Sternwood's daughter, I'd leave her strictly alone. I would think of my job first."

52

Lepski looked pityingly at him.

"You're kidding yourself. She even turned me on, and I was with her for less than ten minutes. I bet he was with her last night!"

"So maybe, but that doesn't prove a thing. I know the guy. I've done insurance business with him. He would no more rip a hooker than I would. So okay, maybe he and the girl were screwing. Where does that get us?"

Lepski frowned, pulling at his underlip.

"After leaving her, he could have walked right into the killer, and is too scared to explain why he was on the murder scene. Anyway, who knows what goes on in a man's mind? He could have flipped his lid and ripped the girl."

"So what do we do?"

"We'll report to the Chief." Lepski was burning for action. "If he gives us the green light, then we talk to Brandon and take him apart."

"Shouldn't we check on these other three guys who own golf ball jackets? Jacoby asked.

Lepski regarded him.

"One of these days, Max, you'll make a good cop. Do you imagine I wasn't going to do just that thing?"

"Who are they?"

Lepski consulted the list Levine had given him.

"Sam Macree: the deputy commissioner of works. He's been in New York for the past week. We can rule him out. Harry Bentley, the golf pro. We'll check where he was last night, but it'll be a waste of time. I know Harry: not the type. Then there's Cyrus Gregg." Lepski frowned, then shook his head. "Didn't he get killed in a road crash around five months ago? He was in real estate and made a load of money. We can rule him out." Lepski thumped the steering wheel. "It all points to Brandon!"

"I remember Gregg," Jacoby said. "He was a snappy dresser. What would his wife have done with all his clothes?"

Lepski stared at him.

"Yeah . . . a good question. I'll check on Harry Bentley.

53

You find out what happened to Gregg's clothes, then we'll talk to the Chief.''

He started the car engine.

"I'll walk," Jacoby said and got out of the car. He watched Lepski drive away, then he walked back into Levine's shop.

"Could you tell me when Mr. Gregg bought his jacket?" he asked as Levine hurried forward.

"That I do know. The poor man wore it on the day he died," Levine said. "A real tragedy! Such a nice man! It was seven months ago. He came in here and bought the jacket. The next morning as he was driving to his office, some kid in a stolen car hit him. They were both killed. A tragedy!"

Jacoby now remembered the details.

"I was wondering what happened to the jacket," he said.

Levine shrugged.

"That I don't know. Mr. Gregg bought all his clothes from me. He had many jackets and suits. I guess Mrs. Gregg got rid of them. Now, there's a tragedy! I tell my wife, money isn't everything. Mr. Gregg had a great deal of money, but he had trouble with his wife and with his son."

"What kind of trouble?"

"Don't let this go further, but Mrs. Gregg is a very difficult lady. Mr. Gregg and I were friends. There were times when he confided in me. Their son meant more to Mrs. Gregg than Mr. Gregg did. It sometimes happens." Levine shook his head. "Mr. Gregg was a good man. Maybe he was too good. When the son was born, Mrs. Gregg switched all her affection to him. Mr. Gregg was a vigorous man." Levine grimaced. "No sex, you understand. I told him he should get a girl. With all his money there would have been no problem, but Mr. Gregg was a good Catholic and a good man. He suffered a lot."

Jacoby began to wonder if he was wasting time listening to all this.

"Tough. What does the son do?"

"I know nothing about him. He doesn't buy his clothes here. I have never even seen him."

"We want to trace this jacket. Maybe Mrs. Gregg can tell us what she did with it."

"Be careful with her. She is very difficult, and she has lots of money. She won't like police officers calling on her."

"Where do I find her?"

"When Mr. Gregg died, she sold the big house. She lives on Acacia Drive: a small place, but nice."

Jacoby decided he would write a report and let Lepski handle this. He thanked Levine, then walked back to police headquarters.

*　　　　*　　　　*

Ken Brandon faced Karen, his heart pounding.

"Are you sure?" he asked huskily. "Are you quite sure?"

"I'm sure. It was the same creep we ran into last night. He's cut his hair and beard, but I knew him at once. He came in to check on me, and I could tell by his grin, he recognized me."

Ken felt a wave of panic run through him.

"What do you think he'll do?"

Karen shrugged.

"How do I know? I don't think he'll talk to the police."

Ken took out his handkerchief and wiped his sweating hands.

"He must be planning something! Why else should he come here?"

Karen stared at him. Her hard eyes showed contempt.

"The way you are acting," she said, "you seem to imagine you are the first husband who has screwed around. It happens a thousand times an hour."

"You don't seem to realize how serious this is!" Ken exclaimed, slamming his fist on his desk. "If your father got to know! If my wife got to know! My life would be ruined!"

"Shouldn't you have thought of that before you got hot pants?" Karen asked. "I have work to do," and turning she swish-hipped back to her desk.

Ken stared after her. What a reckless, irresponsible madman he had been! he thought. To have jeopardized his happiness with Betty and his career for a few sordid hours with this hard, self-indulgent bitch!

Then the telephone bell rang making him start.

A woman's voice said, "Mr. Brandon? I'm putting you through to Mr. Sternwood." She sounded as if she were putting him through to the Pope.

Ken drew a deep breath, then Sternwood's booming voice came on the line.

"Brandon? I've been talking to Hyams. He tells me you are doing great! Thought I would have a word. I'm pleased."

"Thank you, Mr. Sternwood."

"Keep up the good work. Tell me, Brandon, how are you getting along with my little girl? I know she can be difficult, but don't stand any nonsense. You're running the office . . . understand? But she's smart, isn't she?"

Ken hesitated. Was this the moment to get Karen transferred to head office? His nerve failed.

"She's doing well, Mr. Sternwood."

"Good. Keep at it, Brandon," and the line went dead.

Ken sat back. He looked at his watch. The time was 17.55. In five more minutes, he could close the office. He looked at his cluttered desk. He had at least another half hour's work to complete before he left for home.

Karen came to his office door.

"I have a date," she said, and smiled at him. "See you tomorrow and don't look like the prophet of doom. It doesn't become you. 'Bye now," and she walked to the counter, lifted the flap and started for the entrance door as it swung open and Lu Boone came in.

Karen stopped short. She felt her heart skip a beat, but she switched on her sexy smile.

"We're closed for the day," she said. "Could you come back tomorrow?"

Lu grinned at her. Now here was a tough cookie, he told himself. He instinctively knew she recognized him.

"It won't wait, baby," he said and closed the door, then half turning, he shot the bolt. "Brandon here?"

"Yes, he's here. Did you want to see him? I don't have your name."

"Call me Lu," Boone said, lounging forward. "I want to see him and you. Did he give you a good lay last night, baby?"

Sitting at his desk, listening to this conversation, Ken turned cold and sick with panic, then with an effort, he pulled himself together. Moving swiftly, he opened a desk drawer, switched on the tape recorder he used when talking to clients, then half closed the drawer. He got to his feet and walked to the door.

"Here is Mr. Brandon," Karen said. She turned and looked at Ken. "This is Lu. He wants to talk to us."

"Hi, bud!" Lu said, and grinned. "Did she give out last night?"

Ken said huskily, "I don't know what you are talking about. What do you want?"

"Don't feed me that crap," Lu said, his voice toughening. "You know. What do I want? Let's all sit down and talk."

Ken moved back into his office and Lu followed him. Karen remained at the doorway.

Lu looked around.

"Not much of a dump, but I like your home, bud . . . real nice." He sat down on one of the upright chairs. "Come on in, baby. Let's all be sociable."

Ken moved around his desk and sat down. Karen, looking relaxed, moved into the office and leaned against a filing cabinet.

"Is this a hold-up?" she asked. "Or are you high?"

"Don't act too smart, baby," Lu said. "I know all about you. I've been talking around. I know all about you, bud." He grinned at Ken, then at Karen. "Last night, a hooker got killed right by your love nest, baby. I was looking for Paddler's Creek, and you two directed me. I have a good memory for faces. I know you two didn't kill this hooker, but I do know you were screwing in that cabin. This morning the fuzz talked to me. I don't dig that. It seems the fink who killed this hooker got blood all over his clothes so the fuzz went through my things. I don't dig that either. They can't pin the killing on me, so they are looking elsewhere. They wanted to know if I had seen anyone at the time of the killing as I was walking to the camp." He grinned. "I don't give information to the fuzz. I told them I hadn't seen anyone." Again he grinned. "I guess I did you two a big favour. If I had told them I had seen you, you would have them around you like flies, and the word would have got out that you two had been screwing. I didn't tell them, so you owe me for a favour." He paused, looking first at Karen and then at Ken. "I do something for you, you do something for me . . . right?"

Neither Karen nor Ken said anything.

"That's the way I see it," Lu said, after a long pause. "I've been bumming around, living rough, for sometime. I'm changing my life-style. I want money. Now you, bud, have a nice wife. I know all about her, working for this guy who fixes abortions. You, baby, have a rich pa. I know all about him. I guess between us three, we can work out a deal that would put me on easy street, and save you two problems. You with me so far?"

So it was to be blackmail, Ken thought. He glanced down at the half open drawer. He could see the spools of the recorder revolving and was thankful he had had the presence of mind to have switched on the recorder. He looked at Karen who appeared to be completely relaxed. She shrugged.

"Well now," Lu went on, "I decided I wouldn't talk to the fuzz. Now, just suppose, you two tell me to jump in a lake? Maybe, I told myself, you two could be dopey enough not to want to return favour for favour. You two have a lot to lose, so here's my proposition. Give me ten thousand dollars and I leave the scene. No problems for you: no problems for me. Do we have a deal?"

"You get no money from us, you stinking creep!" Karen said before Ken could say anything.

"Sure. I reckoned you would act stupid. So okay, I put on

the pressure." He took from his shirt pocket two slips of paper. "What do you think of this?" He leaned forward and put one of the slips on Ken's desk, then getting to his feet, gave Karen the other slip.

Ken read what was written on his slip.

Mrs. Brandon.
Ask your husband what he was doing on the night of the 22nd with Karen Sternwood in her cabin at Paddler's Creek.
from a well wisher who doesn't believe in adultery.

Karen's slip read:

Mr. Jefferson Sternwood.
Ask your daughter what she was doing on the night of the 22nd with your employee, Ken Brandon in her cabin at Paddler's Creek.
from a well wisher who doesn't believe in adultery.

Lu began to drift to the door.

"I guess you two will want to talk this over together," he said. "I'll contact you in three days. Have the money here: ten thousand bucks. If you are stupid, I mail the letters." He grinned, nodded, then walked away.

Neither Ken nor Karen moved until they heard the outer door slam. Then Ken, white faced, pressed the stop button on the recorder.

"It's his word against ours," Karen said. "You've recorded what he said?"

"Yes."

"Okay. We'll fix this creep. Give me the tape and I'll go to the police."

"What are you saying?" Ken exclaimed. "They'll charge him with blackmail, and he will talk. You and I will become Miss X and Mr. X, but everyone will know!"

Karen cocked her head on one side as she stared at him.

"Are you saying we are going to pay this creep ten thousand dollars?"

"I haven't ten thousand dollars!"

"Nor have I, so we don't pay him. Let him send the letters! My drag of a father will flip his lid, but he's always flipping his lid. I can handle him. He won't want to believe you screwed me, so I can convince him." She looked at her watch. "I'm late for my date. You fix your end. Your wife won't want to believe this either, will she? So it's up to you to convince her. See you tomorrow," and with a wave of her hand, she left him.

Convince Betty? Ken thought. That would mean lying to her. When she got the letter, she would show it to him. Ken knew he could never lie convincingly to her. He had never lied to her in their four years of happy marriage.

He began to pace around his desk. What a mad fool he had been! Remorse, panic, self-disgust tore at him. Then he pulled himself together. What was done, was done! There was only one decent thing to do. He must tell her before the letter arrived. He must hope that her love for him would survive the shock. But suppose it didn't? Suppose she was so shocked, her love for him died? He couldn't bear to think of that possibility. He tried to assure himself that they were too close, but he did realize that their future relationship might never be the same. The thought sickened him, but whatever happened, he told himself, he must tell her: rather than lie to her.

He looked at his watch. The time was 18.30. She would be home now. He would go home at once and tell her.

He locked the office, got in his car and edged into the home-going traffic. The drive back to his house seemed endless. It was stop-start all the way.

Sitting in the air conditioned car, he tried to think what he would say to her: how best to soften his confession? What words did a man use to tell his wife that he had been unfaithful to her?

He was still undecided when he drove into his garage. Betty's car was there.

Bracing himself, he walked into the lobby.

"Ken?" Betty appeared in the doorway of their bedroom.

"Oh, darling! I'm so glad you are back! I was just going to call you."

He could see she was pale and her eyes anxious.

God! he thought. Has that creep been to see her? His heart began to hammer.

"What is it, honey? Something wrong?"

"Mother's just called. Dad has had a heart attack. She wants me."

Betty's parents lived in Atlanta. Her father was a successful attorney, and Ken was fond of him. This news gave him a jolt. His own problem was forgotten.

"Is he bad?"

Betty fought back tears.

"I'm afraid so. Will you drive me to the airport? There's a plane leaving in an hour. I must catch it."

"Of course . . . I'm terribly sorry."

"I'm all packed. Let's go!"

He took a suitcase she handed to him.

"Are you all right for money?"

"Yes . . . yes. Let's go!"

As they drove fast to the airport, Betty said, "I hate leaving you, Ken. I don't know how long I'll be away. Do you think you can manage? There's plenty of food in the freezer."

"Of course. No problem. I wish I could come with you." He put his hand on her. "Not to worry, honey."

Betty dissolved into tears.

He drove on. His mind switched to his own problem. It was unthinkable to tell her now. If she stayed away a week or so, then when the letter arrived, he would destroy it!

He had a reprieve!

*   *   *

Chief of Police Terrell, sitting behind his desk, smoking his pipe, listened to Lepski's report.

"Harry Bentley is in the clear," Lepski concluded. "He was at the club house all the evening. I've seen his jacket, no

61

buttons missing. So that leaves Brandon and Gregg. It's my guess Brandon was with the Sternwood girl, and after screwing her, he came on the body. He could have seen the killer. He could even have killed her. So what do I do? Do I put pressure on him?"

"Check his jacket," Terrell said. "Find out what he says he was doing at the time of the killing. I don't see a man like Brandon being a sex ripper. It's none of our business what Sternwood's daughter does. We have to tread carefully, Tom."

Lepski shrugged.

"Gregg is dead, but he had a lot of clothes. What happened to them? If his wife gave them away, the jacket could have been worn by the killer. From what I hear, Mrs. Gregg is tricky."

"You can say that again, but talk to her. Handle her with kid gloves. She has money and influence, but talk to her."

The time now was 20.15. Lepski decided that Brandon would be home, so with Jacoby at his side, he drove to Brandon's bungalow.

Back from the airport, Ken was trying to relax. He didn't feel like getting himself a meal. He pushed Lu Boone out of his mind and was thinking of Betty's father when his thoughts were interrupted by the sound of the front door bell.

Getting to his feet, hoping it wasn't a neighbour dropping in, he opened the front door.

The sight of Lepski and Jacoby shocked him. He stepped back, his heart beginning to pound, knowing his face had turned white.

Lepski noted the signs of panic, and in his cop voice, said, "Mr. Brandon? Detective Lepski. Detective Jacoby. We want to talk to you."

Ken struggled to control himself. He stood back and said huskily, "Come on in. What is it?"

Lepski and Jacoby followed him into the lounge. Lepski looked around, approving the comfort of the room.

"What is it?" Ken repeated.

Lepski believed in the slow approach. He saw that Brandon was already unnerved: no harm in turning the screw.

"Nice place you have here, Mr. Brandon."

Ken didn't say anything. He stood motionless, looking from Lepski to Jacoby and back to Lepski. He felt a trickle of cold sweat down the side of his face.

Lepski let the silence prolong.

Finally, Ken said, "What is it?"

"We are investigating a murder, Mr. Brandon." Lepski took from his jacket the golf ball button. "This yours?"

Ken stared at the button lying on Lepski's open palm and felt a rush of cold blood up his spine.

"Is this yours?" Lepski repeated sharply.

"I—I don't think so," Ken said, almost sick with panic.

"Mr. Brandon, this button was found a few yards from the murder scene," Lepski said. "It's an unusual button. We have been checking. Four men, including yourself, bought a jacket from Levine with buttons like this one. We have to check. Have you a jacket with this kind of button?"

Ken moistened his dry lips.

"Yes."

"Can I see the jacket?"

God! Ken thought, if there is a button missing!

"I'll get it."

"Thank you, Mr. Brandon," and as Ken went down the corridor to the bedroom, Lepski winked at Jacoby. "He's our guy," he said under his breath.

Opening the closet door in his bedroom, Ken took out the jacket. Feverishly, he checked the buttons, then drew in a long deep breath of relief. No buttons missing! He stood for a minute or so, forcing himself to relax, then he walked back to the lounge and handed the jacket to Lepski.

"There are no buttons missing," he said, his voice much more in control.

Lepski checked the jacket. He was too good a detective to show his disappointment.

"Fine, Mr. Brandon. We have to check these things out.

Sorry to have troubled you."

Ken nodded, feeling a surge of relief.

"Of course."

Lepski gave him his cop stare.

"This girl was killed last night around eight and ten. Where were you at that time, Mr. Brandon?"

Panic again gripped Ken.

"Eight and ten last night?" he repeated to gain time. He had to lie. He couldn't tell this hard faced cop that he was with Karen. He had to protect her and himself.

"That's what I asked," Lepski said, knowing Brandon was thinking up a lie.

"I was home," Ken said. "I should have been at my sister-in-law's wedding anniversary, but my car broke down. I called my brother-in-law and explained."

"What time did you call your brother-in-law, Mr. Brandon?"

"Just after eight. No, it was nearer half past eight."

"Could I have your brother-in-law's name?"

"Jack Fresby, the corporation lawyer."

"Yeah, I know him," Lepski said. "You stayed home the rest of the evening?"

"I was here when my wife returned just after midnight."

Lepski again stared at him, then nodded.

"Okay. Sorry to have troubled you." Lepski gave him his wolfish smile and left.

As he got into his car, he said to Jacoby, "He was lying his head off."

"Wouldn't you?" Jacoby said. "Did you imagine he would tell you he was with the Sternwood girl?"

"He could have seen the killer. I'll talk to him again." He started the engine. "Let's go talk to Mrs. Gregg . . . could be fun."

After a ten minute drive, they arrived on Acacia Drive where the retired rich lived. On rising ground, at the back of the City, all the villas had a direct view of the distant sea and beach. Each villa was individually designed. All of them had at least an acre of garden, hidden from view by ten foot high hedges. Silence reigned over Acacia Drive. The owners were enormously wealthy and old. There were no sounds of transistors: no shouts from the young.

"Like a goddam graveyard," Lepski said, as he drove along the sand-strewn road, looking for Mrs. Gregg's villa.

He found the villa at the far end of the road. Pulling up, he and Jacoby got out and surveyed the massive oak, nail studded gates that hid the villa.

"The way these old farts live," Lepski snorted, and shoving open one of the gates, he peered at the immaculate garden, ablaze with flowers, then looked at the two storey villa, painted white and blue, that stood at the end of the short drive.

Together, the two detectives walked up the drive and paused before the white painted front door. Lepski thumbed the bell, then paused to look right and left. To his right, he saw a big swimming pool. To his left a four car garage. One of the garages contained a Silver Shadow Rolls. The other three garage doors were closed.

The evening sun was hot. They waited for some minutes, then Lepski, muttering under his breath, rang again.

The door swung open, and they were confronted by the nearest thing Lepski had seen out of a horror movie. Here was a tall, emaciated looking man, dressed in black, wearing a wasp waistcoat, black and yellow stripes, with the dignity of an Archbishop.

Lepski gaped at him.

Around seventy years of age, this man had a long, yellow complexioned face, his thinning hair was snow white. His eyes were as expressionless as sea washed pebbles. His lips were paper thin. As he regarded Lepski, his shaggy eyebrows lifted.

"Mrs. Gregg," Lepski said in his cop voice.

"Mrs. Gregg doesn't receive at this hour, sir," the man said in a voice that could have come from the grave.

"She'll see me," Lepski said and flashed his badge. "Police."

"Mrs. Gregg has retired to bed. May I suggest you return tomorrow at eleven o'clock?"

Lepski leaned against the door portal.

"Who are you?" he asked.

"I am Reynolds, sir. I am Mrs. Gregg's butler."

"Maybe we don't have to disturb Mrs. Gregg," Lepski said. "We are investigating a murder." He took the golf ball button from his pocket and showed it to Reynolds. "Recognize this?"

Reynolds regarded the button, his face expressionless.

"I have seen a similar button. The late Mr. Gregg had a jacket with golf ball buttons."

"What happened to the jacket?"

"I had the unhappy task of getting rid of all Mr. Gregg's clothes," Reynolds said. "He had a large wardrobe. Madam asked me to get rid of them at his death."

"Including the golf ball jacket?"

Watching him, Lepski saw the grey eyes shift.

"Yes."

Lepski pulled at his nose, sensing that this man was lying.

"What did you do with the jacket?"

"Among many things, I sent it to the Salvation Army."

Lepski stared at him for a long moment.

"When was this?"

"Two weeks after Mr. Gregg's death. Sometime in January."

"Did you notice that a button was missing on the jacket?"

Again the grey eyes shifted.

"No, I didn't notice."

"This button was found within a few yards of the murder scene," Lepski said. "Are you quite sure the button wasn't missing when you gave the jacket to the Salvation Army?"

"I think I would have noticed it, sir, but I didn't examine the jacket closely. I just gave it away with Mr. Gregg's other clothes."

Lepski looked at Jacoby and shrugged.

"Thank you. I don't think we need bother Mrs. Gregg."

Reynolds inclined his head, stepped back and closed the door.

As the two detectives walked back to their car, Lepski said, "I've got a feeling old Dracula was lying."

"He sure looked shifty."

"You check the S.A. tomorrow, Max. That jacket could be remembered."

They got in the car and headed back to headquarters.

Jacoby said suddenly, "I've an idea. With a jacket like that, and these special buttons, a class tailor like Levine would provide a spare set. What do you think?"

"You've got something. Yeah."

Back at their desks in the detectives' room, Lepski hunted up Levine's home telephone number and called him. After talking to Levine, he said, "Thanks a lot. Sorry to have troubled you," and hung up. He grimaced at Jacoby. "Every jacket had a duplicate set of buttons. So that puts us back to square A! I'm beginning to love this goddam case! So, what have we got? Macree is out. He is still in New York. Bentley has a cast iron alibi. So that leaves us with Brandon and the Salvation Army. I still fancy Brandon. So, tomorrow, you check the S.A. and I'll check Brandon's duplicate buttons. If there is one missing, I'll turn on the heat." He looked at his watch. The time was just after 22.00. "I'm going home. Carroll will be flipping her lid."

"Why didn't you telephone that you would be so late?" Carroll demanded when Lepski entered his home.

"What's to eat?" he demanded, stamping into the lounge.

"It must be spoilt now. I have already eaten."

Lepski made a noise like a ship's siren.

"I've been working my ass off all day, and now you tell me I have nothing to eat!"

"Don't be vulgar, Lepski. Sit down, and I'll get you your dinner."

Lepski beamed. He passed his hand over his wife's behind.

"That's talking! What have I got?"

"Keep your hands off me! There's a time and a place for

67

everything. Sit down!''

Lepski took off his jacket, loosened his tie, and sat down. In a few minutes, Carroll put a casserole on the table. It was her usual disaster, but Lepski was hungry. He poked around with a fork at the contents of the casserole, sighed, then forked an over-cooked lump of meat onto his plate. Somehow, the potatoes, carrots and onions were scarcely cooked.

He began to saw up the meat while Carroll sat by his side. He took a mouthful and began to chew.

"There's brandy and wine in this stew," Carroll said. "How do you like it?"

"Could be nourishing," Lepski said manfully. "The gravy is fine. What's the meat . . . goat?"

Carroll bridled. Any form of criticism was fighting talk to her.

"I'll have you know, Lepski, it is the best neck of lamb!"

Lepski continued to chew.

"That's right?" He swallowed, then began to saw up a potato. It flew off his plate and landed on the floor.

"Lepski! You are a disgusting eater!" Carroll said. "The trouble with you is you try to bolt your food. Cut everything up in small pieces. Take time! Decent eaters enjoy their food slowly."

"Where's that fancy meat mincer I bought you?" Lepski asked. "Let's screw it on the table and give this lot the works."

Carroll stared at him.

"You need to see your dentist, Lepski," and getting up, she walked over to the T.V. set and turned it on.

Lepski moaned softly and began sawing the meat into tiny pieces.

Carroll usually had the last word.

four

AMELIA GREGG, stood, hidden, behind the half open door of the lounge and listened to what Reynolds was saying to these two detectives who had arrived so unexpectedly.

Amelia Gregg was a tall, heavily built woman in her late fifties. Her thick hair was dyed as black as a raven's wing. Her round, heavy face could have been chiseled out of stone. Her large black eyes, her short nose and her thin lips indicated ruthless arrogance.

Listening, she flinched when she heard one of the detectives ask about the golf ball jacket, and she flinched again when she heard Reynolds say the jacket had been given to the Salvation Army. The jacket, stained with blood, was at this moment in the basement boiler room, together with her son's blood-stained grey slacks and blood spattered shoes.

Moving from the door to the window, she watched the two detectives walk down the drive, then, her hand on her floppy bosom, she sat down heavily in a lounging chair.

Since her husband had died in the car crash, some months ago, her life had been completely and unbelievably disrupted.

To her shocked rage, her husband had willed his entire estate to their son, Crispin. To prevent litigation, he had cunningly instructed his son to pay his mother any sums of money which Crispin considered her to be worth.

In a *To Be Read After My Death* letter, given her by Gregg's attorney after the car crash, Gregg had taken revenge for the misery she had inflicted on him during their twenty seven years of marriage.

He had written:

Amelia,

There are only two things in your life that have any meaning for you: the complete domination of our son, and money. Since Crispin was born, you have regarded me merely as a bank account, and nothing else. I know that our son has inherited your ruthless greed so I have decided to leave him my entire estate in the hope he will deal with you as you have dealt with me. There is no way that you can revoke my will. Should Crispin die, the entire estate goes to the Cancer Research Institute, and you will receive an income of ten thousand dollars a year.

You will discover that when Crispin realizes he is no longer dependent on you, he will show his true colours as you did to me.

When you read this, I will be dead, but Crispin will be very much alive. Tread carefully, Amelia. He will be a hard task master, and this thought gratifies me. You have been so selfishly obsessed with your power over our son that you have failed to realize that Crispin is not as other men. You will discover the truth of this when he comes into my money.

Cyrus Gregg.

When Amelia read this letter, she burst out laughing. What drivel this old fool had written!

Independent? Crispin? Again she laughed. Crispin was totally dependent on her, and always would be. She had controlled him for more than twenty years with rigid discipline. She hadn't allowed him to go to a school or to an university. He had been educated at home by expensive tutors. The idea of Crispin mixing with immoral, vicious, drug-taking youthful trouble-makers was not to be considered.

At an early age, Crispin had shown a remarkable talent for painting in oils. This she encouraged as, working in a specially constructed studio on the top floor of the enormous house, she was able to be constantly in touch with him.

She was unable to understand nor to appreciate his strange, wild paintings. His skies were black, his moons were scarlet and his seas were orange. An art expert who she had consulted had spent sometime examining dozens of Crispin's landscapes. Because of the big fee that Amelia paid him, he had guardedly said that Crispin had an unusual talent, but he refrained from saying that, in his opinion, these landscapes, in spite of considerable talent, revealed a diseased mind.

What was this drivel that Crispin was not as other men? Again she laughed. *Not as other men!* She knew that! He was a great artist, and he was her son! Of course, he wasn't like other men!

But what her husband had said about her son becoming independent once he had money nagged her. It was a stupid suggestion, but all the same, it nagged her.

She decided to settle this insinuous suggestion once and for all.

She had gone to Crispin's studio to find him not there. Facing her was a big canvas on an easel. The half finished painting was of a woman, lying on orange coloured sand, her legs spread, her arms out stretched, a ribbon of blood coming from her vagina.

Amelia stood transfixed, staring at the painting in horror. Modern art was modern art, but this . . .! Her face hardened. Crispin must stop this kind of thing! But where was he?

She found Reynolds standing in the vast hall.

Reynolds had been in her service for some twenty five years. Her husband had disliked him and had wanted to get rid of him, but Amelia would have none of it. Reynolds had served her faithfully, and he had been good with Crispin. Over the years, she had begun to confide in Reynolds, consulting him how best she could handle her husband, and, as Crispin grew up, how best to handle him.

Reynolds offered advice that suited her. He never made suggestions unless consulted. Later, she was to discover that he was a hopeless alcoholic and, being shrewd, she knew his one hope of survival was to remain her servant, and this pleased her. She never questioned the disappearing Scotch. She had long ago realized she needed him as he needed her.

"Where is Mr. Crispin?" she demanded. "He is not in his

71

studio."

Reynolds regarded her, his eyes, as always, like wet stones.

"He is in Mr. Gregg's study, madam."

Amelia stiffened.

"In the study? What is he doing there?"

Reynolds lifted his shaggy eyebrows. He was a man of few words.

Her face hardening, Amelia walked down the long corridor to her husband's study, pushed open the door and paused in the doorway.

This big, comfortably furnished room had been Cyrus Gregg's retreat. In this room, at a vast desk, he had manipulated his business deals, arranged his real estate transactions and juggled successfully in stocks.

Amelia seldom entered the room, and it came as a shock to see her son seated in his father's executive chair, the big desk covered with documents, stock quotations and various other papers.

"What are you doing in your father's study?" Amelia had demanded, her voice domineering and harsh.

Pencil between his artistic, long fingers, Crispin made a note, then, with a little frown, looked up.

His eyes were the colour of opals: eyes that would give warning to anyone less confident of her power over him than Amelia.

"My father is dead. This is now my study," he said. His voice was low pitched: a metallic voice of a robot.

Amelia felt a little chill run through her. Her son had never spoken to her before in such a voice.

"What do you imagine you are doing?" she blustered. "Now, Crispin, you must leave all this to me. You don't understand your father's affairs. I do. Although your father has foolishly left you his estate, without my help, you won't be able to manage it. Money needs managing. If it interests you, we will work together, but I think it is better for you to continue with your art, and leave the estate to me."

"I leave nothing to you," Crispin said quietly. "You have

had your reign. Now it is my turn, and I have waited long enough!"

Shocked, fury sending blood in a purple flush to her heavy face, Amelia shouted, "How dare you speak to me like this! Crispin! Go immediately to your studio, and remember, I am your mother!"

Crispin put down his pencil, folded his hands on the desk and leaned forward. His opal coloured eyes lit up. There was such a demoniac expression in them that Amelia recoiled.

Her son looked exactly like her uncle, Martin, dead these forty odd years. Staring at him, she felt stricken.

At the age of ten, Martin, uncle on her mother's side, had attempted to sexually assault her. Staring at her son, and seeing the frightening resemblance, she vividly recalled the happening. Her parents had gone off for the day to some social affair. Uncle Martin, they told her, would take her out to lunch. This had delighted her as Uncle Martin, although eccentric, was fun. He was tall, slim with corn coloured hair, so much like Crispin. He used to dabble in art and dressed even in those days eccentrically. His preference was white frilly shirts and bottle green velvet suits. He was often suspected by his friends to be gay, that was far from the truth. He had a sexual compulsion for young girls, but at the age of ten, Amelia thought he was dashingly romantic.

On his arrival, and after the coloured butler had left them together, Uncle Martin had asked her where she would like to be taken for lunch. Even at that age, Amelia had developed the taste for luxury. She named the most expensive restaurant in the City. There was a strange expression on her uncle's face as he agreed.

"Pretty little girls who ask for expensive outings must give as well as take," he said, and with a fixed smile that turned him into a terrifying stranger, he caught hold of her. The next few moments still remained a nightmare to Amelia. At the age of ten, she was sturdy. As his hand thrust up her dress and between her thighs, she had lashed out at his face. Her wild screams had brought the butler and the footman into the room. They had great difficulty in dragging Uncle Martin away from her. While the struggle went on, Amelia fled to her bedroom and locked herself in. Sometime later, the footman who was on friendly terms with her had told her that Uncle Martin had been certified, and had been put in an asylum where later, he killed himself. Her parents had said nothing to her, nor did she to them.

Now here was her son, glaring at her, the spitting image of Uncle Martin.

She recalled what her husband had written: *You have failed to realize that Crispin is not as other men. You will find the truth when he comes into my money.*

Looking at her son now she realized that her power over him had gone. As he continued to glare at her, she also realized that he not only had become a stranger, but as mad as Uncle Martin.

"Here. . . ." He picked up a sheet of paper. "Take this and read it. It is for you to decide. Now, leave me!"

With trembling fingers, she took the sheet of paper and went unsteadily to the lounge.

Reynolds, white faced, had been listening at the door. He watched Amelia as she walked into the lounge: her arrogance gone, looking like a fat, drooping old woman of eighty.

He went silently to his room and poured himself a treble Scotch. He drank the spirit in one long gulp. Then he took out his handkerchief and mopped his white, sweating face, stiffened, pulled down the points of his black and yellow waistcoat, adjusted his tie, then walked to the lounge. He paused in the doorway.

Amelia looked up and motioned him to come in.

Reynolds quietly closed the door, advanced and took the sheet of paper she held out to him.

"Read it," she said.

Crispin's instructions had been drawn up by Abel Lewishon, his father's attorney. The instructions stated that Amelia had a choice: she could either remain to take over the running of her son's new home with an income of fifty thousand dollars a year for her services, or if this arrangement was not agreeable to her, she would receive an income of ten thousand dollars a year and live where she liked.

The house was to be sold. All the ten members of the staff were to be dismissed with the exception of Reynolds who would be expected to run the new, much smaller establishment with the aid of a cook/maid who Crispin would supply. Reynold's salary would be increased by one thousand dollars a year. If he didn't agree to this, he was to be dismissed.

"He has gone mad!" Amelia whispered. "He has gone the same dreadful way his uncle went. What am I to do?"

Reynolds thought of all the scotch he could buy with the extra one thousand dollars a year. He thought too of the awful prospects of being unemployed.

"I would suggest, madam, you accept these terms," he said. "May I say, madam, that I have often suspected that Mr. Crispin is far from normal. We can but wait and hope."

For the first time in her married life, Amelia wept.

This conversation, between Amelia and Reynolds had taken place some six months ago. During these months, the big house had been sold. Crispin, Amelia, Reynolds and a thin, elderly coloured woman named Chrissy had moved into a villa on Acacia Drive. The villa had been found and purchased on Crispin's behalf by Lewishon.

Although prejudiced, Amelia had to admit that the villa was a success. She had a bedroom and a sitting room on the ground floor. Reynolds had a bed/sitting room, also on the ground floor to the rear of the villa. Chrissy had a small bedroom, leading off the kitchen. The whole of the top floor was taken over by Crispin. He had a bedroom, a big living room and a bigger studio. An oak door, at the head of the stairs, leading to his apartment, was kept locked. Only Chrissy was allowed up there to clean once a week.

Chrissy was a deaf-mute. Neither Amelia nor Reynolds could communicate with her, and Amelia suspected that Crispin had deliberately engaged this woman because of her affliction. She did her work and was an excellent cook, and in her spare time, she was content to watch T.V., only going out to do the marketing. Reynolds guessed she could lip-read. He warned Amelia to be careful what she said to him when Chrissy was around.

Amelia only caught occasional glimpses of her son. For the past months neither had exchanged a word. Outside the locked door leading to Crispin's apartment was a table. Reynolds had been instructed to take up Crispin's meals on a tray, knock on the door, then go away. Crispin ate very little. His lunch consisted of a fish salad or an omelette, his dinner a small steak or the breast of a chicken.

From time to time, he left his studio and drove away in the Rolls. Watching from behind the curtain, Amelia assumed he was going to see Lewishon. She also assumed that when Crispin was locked in his studio, he was painting.

By now she had accepted the bitter fact that she no longer had any power over her son, but at least she had fifty thousand dollars a year, spending money. She had always lived an active, sociable life. She was an expert bridge player. In her big circle of friends, the news had got around that Crispin had inherited his father's fortune. Eyebrows had been raised when the big house had been sold. Amelia had explained that Crispin had become a great, dedicated artist. On no account was he to be disturbed. She had hinted that Picasso might have a rival. Her friends secretly jeered. She was often invited to her friends' homes for cocktails or dinner. As a *quid pro quo*, she invited them to one of the many luxury restaurants in Paradise City, again explaining that Crispin was so sensitive, she could now no longer entertain at home.

But she kept wondering what Crispin was doing, locked away, month after month. Her curiosity became so over-powering, she decided she must find out. One day, she had the opportunity. Chrissy had gone out, shopping. Crispin had already driven away in the Rolls. She called Reynolds.

"Do you think you could get in up there, Reynolds?"

"I believe so, madam. I have already examined the lock. I

could arrange it."

"Then let us go at once!"

It took Reynolds only a few minutes, with the aid of a stiff piece of wire to unlock the door, and together, they entered the studio.

It was like walking into a nightmare world of revolting horror.

Hanging on the walls were big canvasses of such ghastly scenes that Amelia turned faint. The theme of these realistic paintings were always the same: a naked girl, depicted with astonishing photographic detail, lying on a beach with a red blood moon, a black, threatening sky and an orange beach. The girl was either decapitated or disemboweled or hacked in pieces.

In a corner of the room stood an easel on which was a large portrait, completely life-like, of Amelia. Between her blood-stained teeth hung a pair of male legs, clad in white and red striped trousers—her husband's week-end casual dress. From her black dyed hair, sprouted a pair of fur covered horns.

For a long moment, Amelia stared at the painting, then half fainting, she allowed Reynolds to support her down the stairs.

Leaving her in the lounge, Reynolds walked unsteadily to his room and drank a big Scotch. Then, revived, but still shaken, he returned upstairs and relocked the apartment door.

He entered the lounge and poured Amelia a stiff brandy.

"What are we going to do?" she asked, after sipping the drink. "This is dreadful! He is utterly mad! He could be dangerous!"

Again Reynolds thought of the nightmare his life would become if he lost this sinecure of a job.

"I think, madam, there is nothing we can do but wait and hope."

Amelia, thinking what life would be like to live on a mere ten thousand dollars a year, nodded agreement.

So they waited, but without any hope.

Then on the evening after Janie Bandler's murder,

Reynolds made a horrifying discovery. He went immediately to where Amelia was watching T.V. after an excellent dinner.

"Madam," he said huskily, "I must ask you to come with me to the boiler room."

"The boiler room?" Amelia stared at him, then seeing his white, sweating face, she felt a stab of fear. "What is it?"

"Please, madam, please come," and he turned and began walking down the corridor. After a moment's hesitation, now feeling dread, Amelia followed him down the stairs and into the boiler room.

"Look, madam," Reynolds whispered, and pointed.

Amelia regarded the heap of clothes lying by the furnace. She recognized her husband's golf ball jacket which Crispin had taken a liking to and often wore, also Crispin's grey slacks, his blue and white check shirt and his suede shoes. She stared with mounting horror at the unmistakable blood stains. There was a sheet of paper pinned to the jacket. In Crispin's artistic writing was the message:

Destroy these clothes immediately.

They looked at each other, then Amelia turned and stumbled up the stairs and back into the lounge. Reynolds hurried into his room and poured himself a vast Scotch. He swallowed the drink, then went unsteadily to the lounge.

Amelia was staring, transfixed at the T.V. screen. Pete Hamilton was talking. Like statues, Amelia and Reynolds listened to Hamilton's lurid description of the finding of Janie Bandler's mutilated body.

"Someone must be shielding this maniac," he concluded. "His clothes must be heavily blood stained." To Amelia, Hamilton seemed to be staring directly at her. "I earnestly ask whoever it is who is giving this dangerous maniac sanctuary—whether wife, mother, father or friend—to communicate immediately with the police. This vicious maniac could strike again! Until he is apprehended, no woman in our city is safe."

Shaking, Reynolds turned off the set.

"I don't believe it!" Amelia moaned. "God! If Crispin did

this! No! He would never do such a thing!" Then she recalled those dreadful paintings in Crispin's studio, and she shuddered. "Reynolds! We must say nothing! If he has done this dreadful thing, I couldn't face the disgrace! My friends! They would all desert me! What would my life become? I won't believe it!" Then stiffening, she looked wildly at Reynolds. "Get rid of those clothes! Burn them! Do it now!"

It was at this moment that Lepski and Jacoby arrived.

*　　　　　*　　　　　*

The following morning, Max Jacoby called on Mr. Levine, the tailor and borrowed one of his golf ball button jackets. He then drove to the Salvation Army depot and talked to Jim Craddock who was in charge of distributing the many gifts sent in by the city's rich.

Craddock was emphatic that the jacket had not been sent with Cyrus Gregg's other clothes.

"I would have remembered a jacket like this," he said. "No. I didn't receive it."

"This is important, Mr. Craddock," Jacoby said. "Are you absolutely certain this jacket wasn't among Mr. Gregg's clothes?"

Craddock nodded.

"I am absolutely certain. Mr. Gregg's clothes were so good, I sold them to a clothes dealer and the money went to our fund. They were far too good to give away, and this jacket was not among them."

While this was going on, Lepski drove to Ken Brandon's home. He arrived at 08.15.

Ken was preparing to go to the office. Surprised at the long ring on his front door bell, he opened the door to find Lepski.

Panic again gripped him. Ken had imagined since no buttons were missing on his jacket, Lepski would no longer bother him.

"Morning, Mr. Brandon," Lepski said in his cop voice. "I've been checking on these buttons. Mr. Levine tells me he supplied a duplicate set with every jacket. I would like to check the duplicate set you have."

The blood receded from Ken's face.

"Duplicate buttons?" he repeated. "I'm sorry. I can't help you. I don't remember Levine giving me a duplicate set."

"He says he did!" Lepski barked.

"My wife looks after that kind of thing. She's in Atlanta right now. Her father has had a heart attack. She would know. I've got to get to work. When I return home I'll look, but I don't remember any duplicates."

"This is important, Mr. Brandon. Will you look and let me know?"

"Of course I will."

"I'm checking all duplicate buttons. Levine is sure he gave you a set," Lepski went on. "I've checked all the other owners of these buttons and none of the buttons are missing. That leaves you, Mr. Brandon, so let me know."

"I'll do that," Ken said. "I'll call you if I find them."

As soon as Lepski had driven away, Ken went into the living room. Betty kept a big button box. She never discarded anything that might prove useful. His heart hammering, Ken found the box and lifted the iid. Some three hundred assorted buttons were in the box. He turned cold as he saw one of the golf ball buttons among the other buttons. So Levine had given him a duplicate set!

Leaving the box on the settee, he ran into his bedroom and took the jacket from the closet. How he now hated the sight of it! He counted the buttons: three on each sleeve, three on the front: nine buttons! Tossing the jacket on the bed, he returned to the living room and began to hunt through the various buttons. He unearthed eight of the golf ball buttons. One missing! Grabbing hold of the box, he up-ended it, pouring the various buttons on the carpet. Feverishly, he searched, but couldn't find the missing button.

He sat back on his heels, staring at the mass of buttons spread out before him.

Jesus! One missing!

If he told Lepski that one of these goddamn buttons was missing, there would be an inquiry. He might even be suspected of killing this girl! Even if the police didn't arrest him for murder, he would be forced to tell them of his affair with Karen. He shut his eyes, thinking now only of Betty.

With shaking hands, he gathered up the buttons and returned them to the box, then he put the box back on the shelf. He looked at the eight buttons on the settee. He must get rid of them, he told himself. He would swear that Levine had never given him a duplicate set. It would be Levine's word against his! He would have to tell Betty in case the police asked her, and she must support his lie! But what was he to tell Betty? He had to think of some lie to convince her. He tried to think, then the Swiss clock in the lobby chimed nine. He was already late for the office. A lie must come that would convince Betty, he told himself, without hope. Then putting the golf ball buttons in his pocket, he locked the front door and drove to Secomb.

He wasn't to know that as soon as Lepski returned to his desk, he called the Atalanta police. Betty's father, who handled many of the city's court cases in the past, was well known.

"Mrs. Betty Brandon," the desk sergeant said. "Sure . . . she's Mr. Lacey's daughter. He's a good friend of ours. He's pretty sick right now . . . heart. Mrs. Brandon is with him.

"I need a word with her," Lepski said. "Let me have the telephone number."

"Something wrong?"

"No . . . just routine," Lepski said airily.

The desk sergeant gave him the number.

"Don't bother her unless you have to," he said. "Mr. Lacey is real bad."

Lepski grunted, hung up and dialled the number. In a matter of minutes, he was talking to Betty.

"Mrs. Brandon, I'm sorry to trouble you at this time," he said, "but we are trying to trace a set of golf ball buttons. I understand Mr. Brandon has a jacket with golf ball buttons.

I've already talked to him. He can't remember if there was a duplicate set of buttons with the jacket. He said you would know."

Betty had been up all night coping with her parents. Her father seemed to be sinking and her mother was hysterical with grief. This call from the Paradise City police was the last thing she wanted.

"There is a duplicate set," she said curtly. "What is all this about?"

"Just a routine inquiry, Mrs. Brandon," Lepski said smoothly. "Would you know where the duplicates are?"

"In my button box at home. I don't understand. What is this?"

"Thank you, Mrs. Brandon. Sorry to have disturbed you," and Lepski hung up. He looked at Max Jacoby who had been listening in on an extension.

"Now let's see if Brandon dreams up a lie," Lepski said with his wolfish smile.

Hurrying into the office, Ken found three coloured couples waiting patiently. Karen was busy typing. She gave him a jeering little smile.

"Sleeping late these days?" she murmured, without pausing in her typing. "The mail's on your desk."

Ken took the first couple into his office. For the next hour he was fully occupied. Then as the final couple left, he turned his attention to the mail. As he was reading the first letter, the telephone bell rang. Scooping up the receiver, still reading the letter, he said, "Ken Brandon. Can I help you?"

"Lepski, City police," a voice growled and Ken stiffened, nearly dropping the receiver.

"Yes, Mr. Lepski?" He was aware his voice was husky.

"Did you find those buttons?"

Ken drew in a long, deep breath.

"I've been thinking about them," he said, forcing his voice to sound steady. "Mr. Levine must have made a mistake. I am quite sure he didn't give me a duplicate set. I am sure I would have remembered."

82

"No duplicate set, huh?"

"No."

"Are you quite sure, Mr Brandon? As I told you, I am investigating a murder case. I repeat . . . are you quite sure?"

Ken gripped the telephone receiver so tightly his knuckles turned white.

"Yes, I am sure."

"Thanks, Mr. Brandon," and Lepski hung up.

Ken sat for a long moment, staring into space. He was now committed to a dangerous lie. He must warn Betty. Anyway, it was time to telephone her and inquire about her father. He dialled. After a brief delay, Betty came on the line.

"Betty, darling! How's your father?"

"Oh, Ken, he's really bad, but he's putting up a wonderful fight. The doctors say he has a fifty-fifty chance." Betty sounded distracted. "This could take time. I don't know when I can get back. It's mother who is so difficult. I was up all night with her."

They talked for a while. Betty was worried that Ken wasn't eating properly, but he reassured her, then as he began to edge the conversation towards the golf ball buttons, not knowing what he was going to say, the ground was cut from under his feet.

"Oh, Ken! I nearly forgot. I had an extraordinary telephone call about a couple of hours ago from the Paradise police. They were asking about those golf ball buttons on your jacket. They said they had talked to you."

Ken's heart skipped a beat, then began to race. He opened and shut his mouth, but no words came.

"They are asking about a duplicate set," Betty went on. "I told them they were in my button box. What is all this about?"

"I—I'll tell you later," Ken croaked. "Nothing important. I've got someone waiting. I'll call you later. 'Bye, darling. I think of you," and he hung up.

His hand went into his jacket pocket and he fingered the eight buttons. He felt so sick, he was ready to throw up. As he

83

sat, ashen faced, panic gripping him, Karen came in. She paused and stared at him.

"So now what's happened?" she demanded, her voice sharp. "You look like the kiss of death."

Because he had to tell someone, he spilled out the story of the buttons. Karen sat on his desk, swinging her long legs and listened.

"There is one goddamn button missing!" Ken concluded, his voice croaking. "They could arrest me for murdering this girl! Lepski will want to see the duplicate buttons now Betty has told him!" He wiped the sweat off his face with the back of his hand. "I don't know what to do! Then this blackmailer will be here tomorrow!"

Karen regarded him, her eyes contemptuously amused.

"Never mind him," she said. "Tomorrow is another day. Leave this to me." She slid off the desk. "I'll fix it." Then with a snap in her voice, she went on, "Get hold of yourself! Don't lose what guts you have—if any," and hip-swishing, she returned to her desk.

*　　　　*　　　　*

Lepski, itching for action, reported to Chief Terrell.

"Brandon's lying his head off. How about bringing him in and giving him the works?"

Terrell shook his head.

"So he's lying, but that doesn't mean he killed the girl. We could be opening a can of worms if we force him to admit he was with Karen Sternwood. Max has checked the Salvation Army. Craddock is positive the jacket wasn't among Gregg's clothes. I want to find out more about this. Before we do anything about Brandon, I want you to talk to Mrs. Gregg. From what I hear, her butler is a lush. He could have given the jacket to someone. Take it easy with Mrs. Gregg. She draws a lot of water, but make sure you talk to her, and not to her butler."

Lepski drove to Acacia Drive. When he rang the front door

bell, Reynolds, his eyes glazed, opened the door.

"Police business," Lepski said in his cop voice. "I want to talk to Mrs. Gregg."

Listening, out of sight, Amelia braced herself. She walked from the lounge to the lobby.

"What is it, Reynolds?" she demanded in her most arrogant tone.

Reynolds turned.

"A person is here, madam, from the police. He is asking to speak to you."

"The police?" Amelia's fat face was a stoney mask. "Show him in."

Reynolds stepped aside and motioned Lepski to enter. Lepski moved into the lobby and looked at Amelia. What an old bitch! he thought. Imagine having her as a mother-in-law!

"Come in!" Amelia snapped, her voice harsh and she led the way into the lounge. "What is it?"

Moving into the lounge, pausing for a moment while Amelia sat down, Lepski said, "Sorry to trouble you, Mrs. Gregg. We are checking on a jacket with golf ball buttons. It is to do with a murder investigation. Your man told me last night the jacket was sent, with other clothes, to the Salvation Army. I understand Mr. Gregg owned this jacket. Mr. Craddock, who handles all gifts, tells us this jacket was not with your husband's other clothes. We need to know what has happened to this jacket."

Amelia glared at him.

"Of course the jacket was with my late husband's other clothes!" She looked at Reynolds. "That is right, isn't it, Reynolds?"

Reynolds, who had spent some hours in the boiler room the previous night, burning the blood-stained clothing, nodded.

"I have already told this officer that, madam."

Amelia glared at Lepski.

"I know all about Craddock. He is an unscrupulous person! Probably he purloined my husband's jacket for his own use or for the use of his brood of sons. I resent being bothered with this! Now, leave me!"

"This is a murder inquiry," Lepski said. "You are making a serious allegation against Mr. Craddock. Am I to understand that you are saying this jacket was included with Mr. Gregg's other clothes and Mr. Craddock has stolen it for his own use—"

Reynolds had a mild coughing fit, and Amelia saw the red light. Still glaring at Lepski, she said, "All I can tell you is the jacket was given to the Salvation Army. What happened to it is not my affair. The men who made the collection could have stolen it. Anyone could have stolen it. That is your business. All I do know is the jacket was given away." She drew herself up. "If I am bothered further, I will complain to the Mayor who is a good friend of mine."

Lepski gave her his wolfish smile.

"Okay, Mrs. Gregg. Thanks for your time," and he walked by Reynolds and back to his car.

He reported to Terrell.

"Get Max to check out the men who collected the clothes," Terrell said. "You check on Craddock again. We don't want a run-in with that old bitch."

Lepski and Jacoby spent the rest of the day, checking. Jacoby got nowhere with the two collectors. They spent their lives collecting throw-out clothes and they said they couldn't remember anything about any particular article of clothing.

Lepski got nowhere with Craddock.

"I assure you," Craddock said, "this particular jacket was not among the clothes I disposed of."

Lepski believed him. He reported back to Terrell.

"Okay, Tom, leave it for the moment," Terrell said. "Give the boys a hand, checking out these hippies."

*   *   *

Lu Boone lay on his bed, sipping a cup of instant coffee. He had slept late, having spent half the night on the beach with a slim, coloured girl whose technical sexual expertise had surprised him. To-day was Thursday, he told himself. Tomorrow, he would call at the office of the Paradise City Assurance Corporation, Secomb. He had little doubt that he would collect, in cash, ten thousand dollars. Wearing dirty jeans, naked to the waist, he scratched his ribs. What would he do with this money? This problem had been puzzling him. He could, of course, return to college and complete his law training, but that didn't appeal to him: too much grind and too boring. Anyway, a nine-to-five just wasn't on.

A knock on the door interrupted his thoughts. Scowling, he swung his legs off the bed, finished the coffee and crossed the room to open the door.

He was confronted by a tall, grey haired man who held a microphone in his hand.

"Hey, Mr. Boone!" the man said. "I'm Pete Hamilton: Paradise T.V. I've been talking to Chet Miscolo. He tells me you were around here at the time of the murder of Janie Bandler. You could have seen the killer. Is it not a fact that you were passing the murder scene within minutes of the actual murder?"

Standing in the doorway, the sun falling on him, Lu glared.

"Piss off!" he snarled and slammed the door in Hamilton's face.

Behind Hamilton was a small truck which had brought him to the Hippy camp. With a wry smile, Hamilton returned to the truck and slid under the driving wheel.

"Did you get that jerk?" he asked his camera man, concealed in the back of the truck, shooting through a one-way window.

"You betcha," the camera man said.

A couple of hours later, Crispin Gregg turned on his T.V. set and listened to Pete Hamilton's broadcast.

"The police still have no clues leading to the arrest of this sex maniac," Hamilton said. "This morning, I learned that a young man, staying at the Paradise Hippy colony was at the murder scene at the time of the murder. His name is Lu Boone. I tried to talk to him." From Hamilton's face on the screen, the picture dissolved to Boone's cabin. Lu stood in the doorway of the cabin. "Mr. Boone was un-co-operative." Hamilton's voice went on. "I could, of course, be wrong, but I think this young man knows more than he is prepared to admit, not only to me, but to the police."

Crispin studied Lu as he stood in the doorway, then his eyes narrowed and his lips moved into a mirthless smile.

He decided he must do something about Lu Boone. He could be a danger, but even if he was not, he would make a very exciting portrait in oils.

*   *   *

Lepski regarded his paper-strewn desk. He reckoned he had another two hours work ahead of him. He was hungry. He was feeling irritated and frustrated. He would feel better after a good meal and a bath, he decided, and pushed back his chair.

"I'm going home for a decent meal," he told Max Jacoby who was toiling at his desk. "I'll be back in a couple of hours. Okay?"

Max shrugged.

"It has to be, doesn't it?"

In his usual show-off style, Lepski arrived home with screeching brakes and the smell of burning rubber. He always wanted to impress his neighbours, who at this time, would be tending their gardens. He was pleased to see them gaping at his arrival as he stormed into his house. He flung open the door and bawled for Carroll.

Carroll was preparing an elaborate dinner. She had been given a recipe: an affair of chicken breasts done in tarragon and whisky. To her dismay, she found she had no tarragon, but decided this really wasn't important. She also found she had given away Lepski's Cutty Sark whisky. Well, she had mushrooms and a pot of cream. All good cooks improvised, her mother had often told her. So, okay, improvise!

Lepski burst into the kitchen and came to a skidding halt.

"What's to eat?" he demanded. "I've only got a couple of hours before I get back to work."

"You'll eat," Carroll said, more calmly than she felt. Lepski always turned up at the wrong time. "Chicken breasts in a mushroom and cream sauce.

"Hey! Sounds terrific! Soon?"

"Ten minutes. Have you found that sex fiend?"

Lepski blew out his cheeks.

"Not yet." He peered at the chicken, sizzling in the pan. "Yum! Yum! Looks terrific!"

"No clues?" Carroll, who was determined that Lepski was going to be the future Chief of Police, believed all successful police work depended on clues.

"Here and there," Lepski said. "Hurry that bird, honey. I'm starving!"

"I have three very important clues for you," Carroll said, as she added the mushrooms to the pan.

Lepski reared back as if he had trodden on a viper.

"Clues? Don't tell me you've been visiting that whiskey sodden old hag again?"

Carroll gave him a cold stare.

"Mehitabel Bessinger is not a whiskey sodden old hag! She is a brilliant, shrewd clairvoyant! Remember she gave you two vital clues to that killer last year, and you were stupid enough to ignore them! Remember?"*

Lepski groaned, then dashed into the living room, jerked open the door of the liquor cabinet and found his bottle of Cutty Sark missing. Muttering, he dragged his tie loose, scrumpled it and flung it on the floor.

Carroll appeared in the doorway.

"There are times, Lepski," she said coldly, "when I think you have been badly brought up."

This was such an unexpected attack that Lepski gaped at her.

"Stop acting like a spoilt child and listen to me," Carroll said.

*See *Want to Stay Alive?*

"My Cutty Sark! It's gone!"

"Never mind about that! Anyway, Lepski, you drink too much! Now, listen to me! Mehitabel has solved this sex maniac case. You want to solve it, don't you? You want to become Chief of Police, don't you?"

Lepski walked slowly to an armchair and sank into it. He rested his head in his hands.

"Yeah . . . yeah. So the old rum-dum has solved the case!"

"You are not to call Mehitabel an old rum-dum. Now, listen. She looked into her crystal ball and she has given me three clues. She said first you must look for a blood red moon. Second, you must look for a black sky. Third, you must look for an orange beach. Then, and not before, you will find this maniac."

Lepski lifted his head from his hands and gaped at his wife. "A blood red moon? A black sky? An orange beach?"

"That's what she said."

Lepski released a whistle that could have stopped a train.

"Did she give that out before or after she had emptied my bottle of Cutty Sark?"

"Lepski! Pay attention! Mehitabel can be relied on! You now have three vital clues," Carroll said. "It's up to your intelligence to use them."

"Yeah." Lepski sank back in his chair. "Sure. A blood red moon, huh? A black sky, huh? An orange beach, huh?" He closed his eyes and made a noise like a bee trapped in a bottle. "That old hag certainly dishes it out, doesn't she? I could do the same for a bottle of Cutty Sark." Then he stiffened and sniffed. "What's burning?"

Carroll suppressed a scream and dashed into the kitchen.

Fearing the worst, Lepski moaned to himself. Then Carroll called, "Your dinner is ruined! It's all your fault! You talk too much!"

Heavy footed, Lepski walked into the smoke-ladened kitchen and stared at the burned mess in the pan.

"No chicken in mushroom and cream sauce?"

"After all the trouble I have taken!" Carroll began opening

a can of beans. "When will you learn to stop talking?"

"Is that what we are going to eat?" Lepski shouted, eyeing the can of beans. "How about that cold beef in the refrigerator? How about that?"

"That's for Sunday."

"Who the hell cares about Sunday? I'm starving!"

"Don't shout at me, Lepski." But she took the beef from the refrigerator. "Anyway, Lepski, you eat too much."

"Yeah. I've heard that before. So I eat too much. Who the hell cares?"

"Remember the three clues I've given you," Carroll said as she began to cut up the meat. "I know they will solve the case."

"Sure . . . sure. Let's eat for God's sake!"

*   *   *

The time was 23.00.

Ken sat in a lounging chair, more than drunk. He had returned home after work, and was in such a state of panic, he couldn't bring himself to cook a dinner. Any moment, he kept telling himself, there would be a ring at the bell, and Lepski would be there to quizz him about the missing button. He had taken a bottle of Scotch from the liquor cabinet, poured himself a big drink and had sat down to wait.

He would have to tell Lepski the whole sordid story. He was sure the story would leak. Then there was Boone. He was sure Boone would post the blackmailing letters. It was all very well for Karen to say she could handle her father, but he was sure Sternwood would get rid of him. Then there was Betty!

He took another drink.

His life had come to a standstill. It was in ruins!

Then he heard the door bell ring.

Lepski!

He got unsteadily to his feet. The end of his road, he told himself.

He walked from the living room, into the lobby, and

bracing himself, he opened the front door.

Karen said, "Let me in quick. No one has seen me," and she pushed by him as he hastily shut the front door.

He stared at her.

"What are you doing here?"

"Man! Have you been drinking!" Karen said, and hip-swished into the living room.

She was wearing a tight-fitting, emerald green frock. Her breasts pointed at him as he stood in the doorway, bewildered and trying to focus.

"What is it? Why are you here?"

"Look." She held out her hand. In her palm was a golf ball button.

Ken peered.

"That's what you want, isn't it?" she said, smiling at him. "I told you I would fix it."

Ken came into the room. The sight of the button, lying on her palm, slightly sobered him.

"Where did it come from?"

She laughed.

"No problem. I went to Levine's shop. They were busy. I cut the button off one of his jackets, then I walked out. They didn't even notice me. No problem. They'll think the button fell off. Pleased?"

Ken reached for the button. He suddenly felt ten years younger.

Her fingers closed over the button as she continued to smile at him.

"Where's your bedroom, Ken? Let's celebrate," and with a quick movement, she was out of her dress, standing, naked before him. "A button for a screw," she said. "Fair enough?"

Ken looked at her.

Just for a brief moment he reminded himself this was Betty's home as well as his. The bed was Betty's as well as his. The Scotch destroyed these reminders. He saw only this beautiful, sensually built body.

Catching hold of her, he guided her along the corridor to the bedroom.

five

THE SOUND of persistent ringing on his front door bell brought Ken abruptly awake. As he sat up, what felt like a hammer crashed inside his head. He groaned, clutching his head in his hands. He threw off the sheet as the ringing of the bell persisted, swung his feet onto the bedside mat, still holding his head, his eyes shut.

The bell continued to ring, driving hot wires through his head.

God! he thought, I must have been good and drunk last night! Who the hell is this? What's the time?

He forced his eyes to open. Sunshine was streaming into the room. His eyes went to the bedside clock. 08.15!

As he staggered to his feet, his head expanded and contracted and again he released a groan.

Goddamn that bell!

He found he was naked. He reached for and put on his dressing gown.

"What's the excitement about?" Karen asked from the bed.

He spun around and stared at her. She was sitting up, naked, and blinking in the sunshine.

A wave of horror ran through him. Last night came into focus. He now remembered she had given him the button and they had gone to bed together. He had been far too drunk to remember what happened, but he could guess. What the hell was happening to him? To have taken this little bitch into Betty's bed! The horror of doing such a thing sobered him.

"Someone's at the door," he said feverishly. "Get out of

sight!"

"Poor Kenny," Karen jeered as she slid out of bed. "Always in a panic."

He went unsteadily down the corridor and jerked open the front door. Standing on the doorstep was Lepski, with Max Jacoby behind him.

Ken stared at them. The hammer inside his head increased its blows. He was suddenly wildly angry.

"What the hell do you want?" he shouted.

Lepski looked him over. Boy! he thought, has this creep had a night out!

"Sorry to disturb you, Mr. Brandon," he said in his cold, cop voice. "I want to talk more about those golf ball buttons."

Ken fought down his fury. He had to be careful. In a milder voice, he said, "I was going to call you this morning. I've found the buttons. Look, I'm late. I overslept. I have to get to work."

Lepski squinted at him.

"You found them?"

"They were in my wife's button box. I looked and found them."

Lepski made a suggestive move forward.

"Can I see them, Mr. Brandon?"

Ken stepped back, wondering where Karen was. He led the two detectives into the living room, went to the button box, then remembered he had left the buttons in his jacket pocket.

"Wait!" he said, and went to the bedroom. Karen was out of sight. He guessed she would be in the bathroom. He snatched up his jacket which was lying on a chair as Lepski came to the doorway.

Lepski saw at once that two people had been occupying the big bed. Both pillows were indented.

Taking the buttons from the jacket pocket, Ken moved forward, crowding Lepski back.

"Here they are. Now for God's sake, stop bothering me!"

Lepski counted the buttons, then as Ken continued to move forward, he allowed himself to be directed back to the living room.

"They seem to be all here, Mr. Brandon," Lepski said. "I'd like to see the jacket again."

Ken dashed back to the bedroom, snatched the jacket from the closet, then returned to the living room. He thrust the jacket at Lepski.

Lepski counted the buttons, found none missing and was baffled.

"Okay," he said. "I hope I don't have to trouble you again."

"I don't see why you should. You've caused me enough trouble!" Ken snapped.

Lepski gave him his wolfish smile.

"This is a murder investigation, Mr. Brandon. Odd things happen. Do you mind if I take the jacket and the duplicate buttons? I won't keep them long."

"Take them! I don't want to see the jacket ever again! Throw it away!" Ken exclaimed, nearly beside himself.

"You'll feel better after a strong coffee," Lepski said. "I'll return the jacket," and nodding to Jacoby, he let himself out.

Ken slammed the front door and locked it, then he went back to the bedroom.

Karen was dressed and combing her hair before Betty's mirror. The sight of her using Betty's comb sickened him.

"Your little pals satisfied?" she asked.

"I was drunk!" Ken exploded. "I—."

"All right, all right," Karen said and laughed. "Don't vent your guilty conscience on me. You never stopped screwing me all night! I told you the reservoir would fill up."

Ken felt like killing her. He went into the bathroom, slammed the door, shaved hurriedly. Not bothering to shower, he returned to the bedroom and flung on his clothes. He could hear Karen in the kitchen.

"Want coffee?" she called.

He put on his loafers, then went into the kitchen. She had just made a pot of coffee. She poured and sipped.

"Hmm . . . nice. Have a cup?"

"I want you out of here!" he said violently.

"Oh, do shut up!" There was a snap in her voice. "You creeps with hot pants are all the same. Once you've had it, you turn into saints. You'd better get the bed fixed: tell-tale evidence," and she giggled. "Get everything to the laundry." She finished the coffee. "Don't stand there like a constipated camel! Come on! I'll help you."

Ken suddenly remembered the cleaning woman would be arriving at 09.00. He hurried into the bedroom and stripped off the sheets and pillow slips. Using fresh sheets, they remade the bed. He bundled the soiled sheets together.

"Let's get out of here!"

"Look out of the window, dope," she said. "How are you going to get me out without me being seen?"

Ken peered out of the window. His next door neighbour, a retired banker, was pottering in his garden. Ken stood for a moment, panic riding him. How the hell was he going to get Karen away without her being seen?

"Relax," she said. "Come on! I'll get in the back of the car, you put the sheets on top of me, then drive out. Let's go."

That's what they did.

Sweating, Ken waved to his neighbour as he drove out of the garage and then onto the road. When he reached the highway, Karen emerged and sat on the back seat.

Not speaking, Ken finally pulled up outside the office.

"You get started on the mail," Karen said, getting out of the car. "I'll take the sheets to Chan's."

Ken felt helpless. Karen was so overpoweringly efficient. As she walked away, he unlocked the office door and collected the mail. He went into his office and sat down at his desk.

His head still throbbed. He was so sick of himself he just sat there, feeling waves of guilt running through him.

The telephone bell started up. Pulling himself together, he lifted the receiver.

"Paradise Assurance Corporation. Can I help you?"

"Ken?"

The sound of Betty's voice was like a blow under his heart.

"Hi, Betty!" His voice was a croak.

"Darling, Daddy's sinking." Betty's voice was unsteady. "The doctors now say there isn't much hope. He keeps asking for you."

Ken closed his eyes. To him, Betty's father was like his own father. This news drove blood from his face.

"I'll be with you on the first plane out. Oh, honey, I'm so sorry."

"I've checked the planes. There's one at 10.30. Can you make it?"

"I'll make it. I'll rush home and pack a bag. I'll be with you."

"Mary and Jack are coming. I'll be at the airport to meet you. Bless you, darling," and Betty hung up.

Ken got unsteadily to his feet as Karen came in.

"The sheets . . ." Then she stopped and stared at him. "What the hell's the matter now?"

"My father-in-law is dying," Ken said. "He's asking for me. I have to go. I'll try to get back on Monday."

As he started for the door, Karen said, "Aren't you forgetting our little pal, Lu? He's coming today to collect ten thousand dollars."

Ken stared wildly at her, then beside himself, he shouted, "To hell with him!" and ran out to his car.

*　　　　*　　　　*

Fat Katey White sat on the sand before the smouldering fire, her breakfast chores finished. Most of the colony had gone off, either to swim or to hunt for a dollar. She liked this period when the colony was quiet. Before long, Lu Boone would leave his cabin and come for his breakfast. Katey had put aside five sausages for him, and she planned to fry some bread. She regretted there were no eggs.

As she sat there, she thought of Lu. She heard him say again to her: *You'll always be wanted. You have this thing.* No one had ever said such a nice thing to her, she thought, sighing.

97

She knew, of course, it wasn't true, but coming from such a fantastic man, she moaned softly to herself with pleasure. Some men dug fat girls, she thought. It just might be possible that Lu meant it! Just suppose he did mean it? Just suppose he invited her into his cabin! Just suppose he made love to her! She closed her eyes. Only once had a man taken her, and he had been drunk, but Katey still remembered that frightening, but wonderful moment when she came off.

She dreamed on, imagining herself in Lu's strong arms.

"Gone to sleep, Katey?"

She started and looked up. Chet Miscolo stood over her. She liked Chet and she smiled.

"Just dreaming. I'll clear up in a minute."

"What were you dreaming about?" He squatted down on his haunches.

"Private dreams. Don't you dream sometimes?"

"Who doesn't?" He ran his fingers through his bush of hair. "I'm worried, Katey. It's not going to help us being on T.V. I know for sure there was a camera man in that truck yesterday. That guy, Hamilton, is a mischief maker. We could be told to clear out . . . then where would we go?"

"There are always places," Katey said complacently. She had become such a nomad she was happy to settle anywhere so long as she had company, a decent fire to cook on and a supply of sausages and spaghetti. "What's the time?"

"Just after ten," Chet said. "We have been here two years, Katey. It'll be tough if we have to leave."

Katey wasn't listening. In another few minutes Lu would be coming for his breakfast. She wanted to be alone with him.

"Aren't you going for a swim?" Her voice a little too anxious.

Chet grinned.

"Expecting company, Katey? Yeah, I'll take a swim." He stood up. "Boone said he was leaving tomorrow."

"He told me. Maybe he'll come back."

Her expression of resigned despair touched Chet.

"I expect he will," he said gently, knowing that by

tomorrow, they would see the last of Lu Boone. "See you," and he ran off towards the sea.

Katey took the five sausages from the plastic bag and laid them, with loving care, in the pan which she put on the fire. Then she cut some slices of bread and using a little oil, she added the bread to the pan.

He could be out in a few minutes, she thought. Everything would be ready for him.

When the bread was crisp and golden and the sausages browned to perfection, and there was no sign of Lu, Katey began to get worried. She removed the pan off the fire. Maybe, she thought, he was still sleeping. Then an idea occurred to her. She would take his breakfast to his cabin! He was probably dozing on his bed and he would welcome having his breakfast served in bed.

Her heart began to flutter. He just might invite her to stay while he ate.

She hurriedly poured boiling water from the cauldron onto a plate, dished up the sausages and bread, snatched up a knife and fork and walked across the sand towards Lu's cabin.

Pausing outside the door, she timidly knocked. She waited, the hot plate in her hand. She heard nothing. The food was getting cold! She rapped harder. Still she heard nothing. He must be sleeping, she thought. She tried the door handle and the door swung open.

"Lu?" she called. "I have your breakfast."

She peered into the cabin.

Strong sunlight came through the slats of the shutters. The sun lit up the table, facing her. On the table stood Lu's severed head in a circle of blood and festooned with flies.

Katey dropped the plate. The sausages and bread cascaded onto the floor.

Chet Miscolo, walking out of the sea, heard Katey's horrifying screams. Realizing something terrible must have happened, he ran frantically towards Lu Boone's cabin.

A seagull, startled by Katey's screams, cried plaintively and swooped out to sea.

*   *   *

Terry Down, the police photographer, having taken shots of Lu Boone's mutilated body, dashed into the shrubbery to throw up. Even hardened cops like Beigler, Hess and Lepski were glad to leave the cabin and to wait in the hot sunshine for Dr. Lowis and his two interns to take over.

"It's our nut again," Beigler said and wiped his sweating face with his sleeve. "We could be wrong in thinking he's a sex nut: he could be a homicidal nut which means even more trouble."

"Did you catch Pete Hamilton's T.V. talk yesterday?" Hess asked. "Hamilton said maybe Boone had seen the killer, and wasn't talking. That hint might have alerted our nut to fix Boone."

"But why cut him up?" Beigler asked.

"Because he's a damn nut!"

The three men turned as Dr. Lowis came from the cabin.

"What have you got, doc?" Hess asked.

"A mess." Lowis shrugged. "At a close guess, I'd say he was killed around two o'clock this morning. His killer probably knocked on the door and when Boone opened up, stabbed him: an instant killing. The chopping up was done with a broad bladed knife. Again at a guess, the kind of tool sugar cane cutters use. The head was removed with two violent strokes. The rest of the damage shows the weapon was as sharp as a razor."

"Can you get him out of here?" Hess asked. "We want to go over the cabin."

"The boys are fixing him now . . . won't be long."

Lepski said, "I'll talk to Miscolo. The girl who found him is in shock. Can't get a thing out of her."

A second ambulance arrived with screeching sirens.

"I'll put her under sedation and get her to the hospital," Lowis said and hurried off.

Katey lay on the sand, her hands covering her face while

she moaned. Every now and then her heels drummed on the sand while a big crowd of hippies stared down at her. As Lepski walked over to them, Katey was whisked away in the second ambulance.

Chet Miscolo sat on the sand and Lepski dropped down beside him while the rest of the group gathered around.

"He was killed around two this morning," Lepski said. "Did you hear anything?"

"I was asleep . . . nothing. Poor Katey . . . she dug him."

Lepski looked at the group of young people.

"Anyone see or hear anything?"

A tall, thin youth moved forward. His hair stood around his head like a bee-hive.

"I did," he said.

Dusty Lucas had joined Lepski and he took out his notebook.

"Who are you?" Lepski asked.

"Bo Walker. I'm on vacation. Last night, I had to get up for a leak," the youth said. "The time was two forty five."

"How did you know that, Bo?"

"I have a watch, man. When I got out of my sack, I looked at my watch. My old man gave it to me for my twenty first birthday. I like to look at the goddamn thing."

"So you got up for a leak at two forty five . . . then what?"

"There was a light on in Boone's cabin. Okay, I thought, if a guy likes to stay up this late, so he stays up."

"Did you see him, Bo?"

"I didn't see a thing: just the light, but I heard something. I heard two bangs: the kind of bangs a butcher makes with a cleaver when cutting up meat."

"That guessing? How do you know the sound a butcher makes cutting up meat?"

Bo smirked.

"My old man's a butcher."

"This was two forty five . . . right?"

"Yeah."

At least, Lepski thought, he had pin-pointed the time. He

felt sure the two blows Bo had heard was when the head had been severed.

"Then what happened?"

"I went back to my sack. That's it."

"The light was still on when you got into your sack?"

"Sure."

"Can you add to this, Bo? It's important."

"That's it, man."

"You staying long?"

"Sure. Another month. I dig this place."

"I'll want to talk to you again, so stay put. Okay?"

Bo nodded.

"And listen," Lepski went on, his voice serious, "keep this to yourself. Boone got under the limelight, and this killer fixed him. So say nothing to the media. Understand?"

A scared look came into Bo's eyes.

"You think this killer could come after me?"

"Just keep your mouth shut," Lepski said, then looking around at the others, "Anyone else saw or heard anything?"

There was a negative shake of heads.

"Get his home address," Lepski said to Dusty and hurried back to Boone's cabin.

The homicide squad and the fingerprint men were working in the cabin. Hess, standing under a palm tree, smoked a cigar. Lepski told him what Bo Walker had said.

"So, okay, we now know for sure when the guy was killed," Hess said. "That's important." He stared at the cabin. "Maybe the boys will come up with something. Staying in there makes me sick to my stomach. It's a goddamn blood bath, plus flies."

Detective Hayes of the homicide squad came out of the cabin and walked over to Hess. He handed him two envelopes.

"Found these in his duffle bag."

As Hess studied the envelopes, Lepski peered over his shoulder. The first envelope was addressed to Mrs. Ken Brandon. The second was to Mr. Jefferson Sternwood.

Removing the contents, Hess read the extortion notes Boone had shown Ken and Karen.

"So this fink was blackmailing them," Hess said, putting the slips of paper back in their envelopes. "Here's our motive."

"Yeah." Lepski slapped at a mosquito that was buzzing him. "You know, Fred, I can't dig a guy like Brandon doing a cut-up job like this, nor do I see him doing that job on Janie. This is a nut job, and Brandon isn't a nut."

"How do you know? How do you know what goes on in this guy's mind?" Hess said impatiently. "Here is a motive. Take these letters to the Chief and see what he thinks."

Twenty minutes later, Lepski bounded into the Detectives' room. As he came to a skidding stop before his desk, Max Jacoby signalled to him.

"Levine, the tailor, called five minutes ago. He said he wanted to talk to you . . . urgent."

"The Chief in?"

"He's with the Mayor."

Lepski sat at his desk and called Levine.

"Lepski. You wanted me, Mr. Levine," he said when the tailor came on the line.

"Those golf ball buttons, Mr. Lepski," Levine said. "I thought you should know. I've one jacket left. This morning I had a client interested. When I went to the rack, I found there's a button missing on the jacket."

Lepski stiffened to attention.

"The button could have dropped off, Mr. Levine."

"Certainly not! It was cut off!" Levine's voice went up a note. "There's nothing shoddy about my clothes, Mr. Lepski! This button was cut off!"

"I'd like to borrow the jacket for a couple of days."

"I've sold the jacket. I put on another button."

Lepski made a soft whistling noise, controlling his exasperation.

"Who did you sell it to?"

"A gentleman. He paid cash."

103

"Does that mean you don't know his name?"

"He was passing through. He said he was from Texas. Why should I need his name if he paid cash?"

"Mr. Levine, suppose someone cut off the button and put it either on his jacket or among the duplicates you supply, would you know if the button was the original or the cut-off button?"

"How would I know that? A button is a button."

Lepski made a noise like a meat grinder hitting gristle.

"What was that, Mr. Lepski?" Levine asked, startled.

"Okay. Okay. Thanks." and Lepski slammed down the receiver. He explained the situation to Jacoby.

"Take Brandon's jacket and the duplicate buttons to the lab boys," he said. "Ask them to see if the buttons all came from the same mould and at the same time."

When Max had gone, Lepski sat at his desk, thinking, then he called Levine again.

"Just another question, Mr. Levine. Did Mr. Ken Brandon visit your shop within the past two days?"

"Mr. Brandon? No, I haven't seen him for weeks. He is not one of my regular clients."

Lepski sighed.

Well, he thought, at least it was a try. Thanking Levine, he hung up.

It wasn't until 11.45 that Chief of Police Terrell returned to headquarters after a long session with the Mayor.

Beigler, Hess and Lepski joined him in his office.

"Okay, Fred," Terrell said as he lit his pipe. "What have you got?"

"The exact time when the killer cut off Boone's head. As an alibi breaker, it is important, but that's about it. The cabin is full of prints. We are checking each and everyone . . . a big job. It would seem our nut is getting cute. It's my guess, he stripped naked before he cut up Boone: so no blood stains on his clothing. From the look of the shower room, he washed off. There are traces of blood. Then there are those two blackmail notes. They could give us the motive. Brandon, under pressure, could have decided to silence Boone."

Terrell looked at Lepski who was sitting forward, bursting to talk.

"What have you got, Tom?"

Lepski told about Levine's telephone call and about the missing button.

"Brandon could have slipped into the shop when Levine was busy and cut off the buttons. I've sent his jacket and the duplicate buttons to the lab."

"Now, I'll tell you something," Terrell said. "Mayor Hedley wanted to know what we are doing and how far we have got. I told him about Karen Sternwood and Brandon." Terrell grimaced as he puffed at his pipe. "Hedley practically blew his top. His ruling is that unless we come up with irrefutable—repeat irrefutable—proof that Brandon is a nut, we lay off Brandon. Sternwood is backing a big City loan. If we stir up a scandal about his daughter, heads will fall . . . maybe, only one head . . . mine. So we don't put pressure on Brandon unless we get irrefutable proof he is a nut."

"Brandon has a strong motive," Hess said.

"You're forgetting. Pete Hamilton supplied the killer with a motive. He practically said that Boone had seen the killer. There's a possible motive."

"Suppose the lab boys show one of the buttons of Brandon's duplicate set is the cut-off button?" Lepski said. "What then?"

"What does it prove except that Brandon is desperately trying to cover up on his affair with the Sternwood girl?" Terrell said impatiently. "Before we go after Brandon, we have to have much more proof and we don't go after him until we get that proof!"

Hess snorted.

"So we are back to square A."

"No, we're not. We haven't traced Cyrus Gregg's jacket," Terrell said. "Mrs. Gregg and her butler say the jacket was given to the Salvation Army. Craddock swears he never had the jacket. The two collectors don't remember it, but that doesn't mean one of them didn't keep the jacket to give away, wear himself or sell." Terrell looked at Lepski. "Get Brandon's jacket back from the lab and take it to Pete Hamilton. I want the jacket shown on television. I want real heat put on the jacket. Get it photographed and send copies to all the newspapers. It could turn up something."

Lepski brightened. He would fix it with Hamilton that he would show the jacket on the T.V. screen. Carroll would love that! Boy! Would this make his neighbours talk! Detective 1st Grade Lepski on television!

*   *   *

Lieutenant Dave Willenski, in charge of the police laboratory, regarded Lepski with disapproval as Lepski skidded to a stop at his desk.

Willenski was growing old in the service of the police. Tall, thin, balding with bushy eyebrows and a drooping moustache, he was regarded as the best lab man on the Pacific coast.

"The jacket Jacoby delivered," Lepski said briskly. "You finished with it?"

Willenski sat back in his chair.

"The problem was the buttons . . . right?"

Lepski shifted impatiently from one foot to the other.

"Yeah . . . yeah. Never mind the buttons right now. I want the jacket. I'm going on T.V. in an hour with it . . . so let's have it!"

"Jacoby asked me to see if one of the buttons was an odd man out," Willenski said with irritating calmness. "You know something, Lepski?"

Lepski did a double shuffle.

"What?"

"You guys at headquarters don't use your eyes."

Lepski made a noise like a cat being trodden on.

"Never mind. Let's have the jacket!"

"You only use your legs," Willenski went on. "Now, if you

had used your eyes, you would have seen all the buttons have serial numbers."

Lepski stared.

"Is that right?"

"If you had looked closely at the buttons you would have saved me the waste of time to use my eyes."

"Sure . . . okay, so we don't use our eyes. Let's have the goddamn jacket!"

"One of the buttons doesn't belong to Brandon's jacket or his duplicate set. I suggest you check the serial number of this odd button with the remaining buttons on Levine's jacket."

"That could prove that Brandon or someone cut off the button and included it with Brandon's duplicates . . . right?"

"It could prove that, but you had better check Levine's buttons."

"We'll do that. Let's have the jacket."

Willenski smiled. His superior smile was the most irritating smile in the world.

"But it won't prove Brandon is your killer."

Lepski clenched and unclenched his fists.

"So?"

"The button Hess gave me, found on the murder scene has a different serial number. It doesn't match up with Brandon's nor Levine's buttons, so you will be wasting your time."

"So, okay, that's what I'm paid for," Lepski said, thinking only of his appearance on the T.V. screen. "Time's running out. Where's the jacket?"

"The trouble with you guys at headquarters," Willenski said, "is you are always after publicity. When I was a young cop. . . ."

"Yeah. I know: you and Sherlock Holmes. Where's the goddamn jacket?"

Willenski sighed, got to his feet and went to a closet. He produced the jacket which Lepski snatched from him.

"I'll be back," Lepski said, and rushed out of the room. On his way down stairs, he came upon a telephone booth. He remembered he hadn't alerted Carroll. Coming to a skidding stop, he called his home.

When Carroll came on the line, he said, "Honey! Pin your ears back. . . ."

"Is that you, Lepski?"

Lepski made a noise like a shotgun firing.

"Who do you think it is . . . the goddamn milkman?"

"Lepski! Stop swearing and stop making horrible noises! You nearly deafened me!"

"Okay! Okay! Now, listen. . . ."

"You listen to me," Carroll said firmly. "What have you done about Mehitabel's clues?"

Lepski dragged his tie loose.

"The blood red moon? The black sky? The orange beach?"

"I'm glad you are thinking about it," Carroll said. "How far have you got?"

Lepski moaned to himself.

"It's under control. Now listen, honey. . . ."

"What do you mean . . . under control? What kind of talk is that?"

"Will you listen?" Lepski bawled. "I'll be on Pete Hamilton's T.V. show at nine. Me! Do you hear? I will be . . ."

"Oh, Tom!" Carroll's voice turned to honey. "How marvellous! You really mean it?"

"I'm telling you! at nine o'clock! Listen, honey, alert the neighbours! Get moving! I want those finks to see me! Spread the news! Okay?"

"Tom! Of course! Pete Hamilton's show at nine?"

"Yeah. I've got to move. Time's running out!"

"I can't wait!"

Lepski cut the connection, then rushed down to his car and drove to the T.V. studios.

A pert chick at the reception desk gave him a sexy smile.

"Detective Lepski? Sure, Mr. Hamilton is expecting you. Second floor, fourth door."

"Thanks." Thinking of his first appearance on a T.V. screen, he went on, "Do I have to make-up?"

"They'll fix it. You'll have no problems."

Lepski took the elevator to the second floor. He found Hamilton talking to two men in shirt sleeves.

Beigler had already cleared the way with Hamilton on the telephone, and Hamilton agreed to co-operate.

Lepski stood around, holding the jacket, shifting from one foot to the other until Hamilton came over.

"Hi, Lepski!" Hamilton said, regarding Lepski with his cold, cynical eyes.

"Hi, Pete! I'm showing the jacket. We don't want it out of our hands."

"No problem. Okay, let's go."

"Don't I want make-up or something?" Lepski asked anxiously.

Hamilton looked him over.

"You'll be fine as you are. Let's go."

He led Lepski into a brilliantly lit studio where cameras were set-up and a small army of technicians were lolling around.

"I'm putting you on the first spot," Hamilton said. "All you have to do is to hold the jacket. I'll do the talking. Let's have a quick run through." He pointed to a table. "Stand behind that, and hold up the jacket."

"Wait a minute," Lepski said. "Should I wear my hat?"

Hamilton released a sigh.

"All cops wear hats. Sure . . . wear it."

Lepski positioned himself behind the table. Two technicians showed him how they wanted him to hold the jacket. Cameras moved forward. Lepski braced himself. This was his moment!

Hamilton stared, then nodded.

"Okay, relax. I'll give you your cue." He looked at the wall clock. "Coming up." He went over to a chair and sat down. Another camera focussed on him.

Sweating slightly, Lepski waited. He was aware that Hamilton was talking, but his mind was elsewhere. He thought of Carroll, waiting. He thought of his fink neighbours

109

also waiting. Boy! Wouldn't he make a goddamn impression!

Then he heard Hamilton say, "This is the jacket the police want to identify."

A bearded youth signalled to Lepski who wasn't sure what expression he should wear. He decided the stern cop rather than the grinning cop was the thing. He turned on his ferocious expression as the camera zoomed in. The bearded youth signalled him to hold it, and Lepski changed his expression from ferocious to looking friendly.

"Anyone recognizing this jacket," Hamilton was saying, "who has any information, no matter how trivial, about this jacket should contact police headquarters."

The camera moved away. The bearded youth signalled to Lepski it was over, and Lepski folded the jacket and drew in a sigh of satisfaction.

A girl touched his arm and motioned him to the door. Hamilton was still talking. Lepski couldn't care less. He had had one minute of fame. As he walked, feeling ten feet tall, into the impressive lobby, he saw a row of telephone booths. He called home.

After a delay that made him hop from one foot to the other with impatience, Carroll came on the line.

"Hi, baby! How did you like it?"

"Like what?" Carroll demanded, her voice shrill.

"Come on, baby. How did I look?"

"Let me tell you something. I invited the Lipscombs, the Watsons and the Mayfields to watch with me. Right now they are guzzling your Cutty Sark like thirsty camels, and they are already eyeing our last bottle of gin."

"To hell with them!" Lepski shouted. "I want to know how I looked!"

"How should I know?" Carroll snapped. From the tone of her voice, he could tell she was in a raging temper.

"For Pete's sake! Didn't you watch the Hamilton show?"

"Of course we watched it!"

Feeling strangled, Lepski dragged at his tie.

"Then you saw me, for Christ's sake!"

"Don't be blasphemous, Lepski!"

"Did you or didn't you see me?" Lepski bawled. "Were you all so stinking drunk on my scotch you didn't see me?"

"We were not drunk and we didn't see you! All we saw was a close-up of the jacket, held by hands. If they were your hands, you should have washed them. They looked grimy!"

Lepski gave a great start as if he had been goosed by an icy finger.

"Just hands, huh?"

"Yes! I've got to go before they get at the gin bottle. They are having a ball . . . that's more than I am! The Mayfields are throwing hints they haven't had supper! I could have them with me for the rest of the night!"

"Just hands, huh?" Lepski said, dazed. Then he understood why he hadn't been made-up. Why Hamilton hadn't cared if he wore his hat or not. He released a soft hissing sound. "Why the goddamn stinking creep!"

"Get home as soon as you can," Carroll said. "I need help here."

"Yeah . . . yeah. I'll be back as soon as I can," Lepski said, his voice low. A vast black cloud of depression settled over him.

Carroll suddenly softened, recognizing from the tone of his voice, his shattering disappointment.

"Dear Tom, I am so very sorry. You come right home and I'll try to make it up for you."

"Yeah. Okay, honey," and Lepski hung up. He walked, heavy footed, out to his car and headed back to headquarters. He felt as if his ambitious little world had come apart at the seams.

Entering the Detectives' room, he paused to gape. Three men from Homicide were at desks. Jacoby and Dusty were also at their desks: all were talking on their various telephones.

Beigler took the jacket from Lepski.

"Get moving, Tom," he said. "That broadcast really started something. The moment it was off the air, people

111

started calling in. Everyone in the City seems to have something to say about the jacket. We could be here all night."

Lepski heard his telephone bell start up. He plodded across to his desk, sat down, pulled a scratch pad and pencil towards him, then lifted the receiver.

"Lepski. Police headquarters."

"This is Mrs. Applebaum. I've just seen that jacket on the Pete Hamilton show. Mr. Hamilton said to contact the police . . . right?" She sounded a very aggressive lady.

"That's right, madam," Lepski said.

"It is my husband's birthday next week. I find it very difficult to give him a present."

Lepski dug his fingers into the surface of his desk.

"You have information about the jacket, madam?"

"No. I want information from you. The police are supposed to give information . . . right?"

Lepski pushed his hat to the back of his head and dragged at his tie.

"I'm not following you, madam," he said in a strangled voice.

"I want information! I want to buy a jacket just like the one I saw on the telly for my husband's birthday present. Where can I buy it?"

Lepski made a noise that would have frightened a hyena and slammed down the receiver.

six

CLAUDE KENDRICK sat back in his massive, antique chair and released a sigh. His breath fluttered the papers on his desk. In a depressed mood, he looked around his reception room which he refused to call his office although all his big deals and sales were transacted there. It was a vast room with an enormous picture window over-looking the sea, sumptuously furnished with some of his most impressive treasures (anyone could buy them if they had enough money) and paintinrs worth a fortune, hanging on the silk covered walls.

Al Barney,* that doyen of the waterfront, had once described Claude Kendrick as follows: "Let me give you a picture of Claude Kendrick. He is a tall, massively built queer of around sixty years of age. He wears an ill-fitting orange coloured wig and pale pink lipstick. He is as bald as an egg, and wears this wig just for the hell of it. When he meets a lady client he raises the wig like you would raise your hat . . . strictly a character. He is fat: soft, massive fat that is no good to anyone. He has a long thick nose and little green eyes and what with all this fat covering his face, he looks like a dolphin, but without a dolphin's nice expression. Although he looks comic, and often acts comic, he is a top expert in antiques, jewelry and modern art. He runs his gallery on Paradise Avenue, the swank quarter of the City, with the aid of a

*Ear To The Ground & You're Dead Without Money.

113

number of gay boys, and he makes a load of dough."

Apart from his flourishing gallery, Kendrick was also a fence. He became a fence by force of circumstances. Important collectors came to him, wanting some special art treasure that was not for sale. Their offers were so tempting, Kendrick couldn't resist. He found a gang of expert art thieves who stole what his clients wanted and he sold to the clients at a huge profit, and his clients keep the treasures in their secret museums.

On this bright, sunny morning, Kendrick was gloomily reviewing his half year's balance sheet. He was not satisfied. The trouble with his ultra rich clients was that, from time to time, they died. The new generation seemed impervious to his beautiful paintings and antiques. All they seemed interested in were sexy women, drugs, drink and expensive cars.

He had been looking at his long list of rich art collectors, ticking off those alive and those now dead. He had come upon the name of Cyrus Gregg. Now, there had been an excellent client! Kendrick again sighed. He remembered how he had unloaded a doubtful Picasso, a still more doubtful Chagall and many other costly, apparent treasures on Gregg. Since the good man had died so suddenly, the Gregg account had ceased to exist.

While he was ruminating sadly of life and death, his door opened and Louis de Marney, his head salesman, fluttered in.

Louis was pencil thin and could have been any age from twenty five to forty. His long thick hair was the colour of sable. His lean face, narrow eyes and almost lipless mouth gave him the appearance of a suspicious rat.

"Darling! Guess who?" he whispered, fluttering to Kendrick's desk. "Crispin Gregg! He's buying oil paints! Jo-Jo is taking care of him, but I just knew you would want to know!"

Kendrick heaved himself out of his chair, took off his wig and thrust it at Louis.

"Comb it!"

"Of course, pet." Louis produced a comb from his pocket,

ran its fine teeth through the hair of the wig and handed the wig back to Kendrick with a flourish.

Moving to a Venetian mirror—worth thousands of dollars—Kendrick put on the wig, adjusted it, regarded his enormous bulk, straightened his immaculate cream coloured jacket, then nodded to his reflection.

"This is destiny," he said. "At this very moment, I was thinking of his dead father."

He walked into the vast gallery. In the artists' material department, he found Jo-Jo, a young blond, laying tubes of oil paints, as if they were jewels, on a pad of black velvet before a tall, thin man whose back was to Kendrick.

Moving like a Spanish galleon in full sail, Kendrick approached.

"Mr. Gregg!"

The tall, thin man turned.

Kendrick found himself confronted by a man with ash blond hair, cut close. His face was pale: the face of a man who avoided the sun. His features were symmetrical: a long, thin nose, a wide forehead, a full-lipped mouth. All this Kendrick took in at a glance, but the man's eyes not only held him, but startled him: eyes like cloudy opals and as expressionless.

"I am Claude Kendrick," Kendrick said, his voice as smooth as oil. "I had the great pleasure of serving your late lamented father. It is an honour and a pleasure to meet you."

Crispin Gregg nodded. There was no smile, no offer to shake hands: just cold, bored indifference, but this didn't dismay Kendrick. He had so often dealt with rich clients who treated him like a lackey, but eventually spent money with him.

"I was just getting some oil paints," Crispin said.

"I do hope we have everything you need, Mr. Gregg."

"Oh yes." Crispin turned to Jo-Jo. "Wrap them. I'll take them."

"Our pleasure, sir," Jo-Jo said, bowing. He picked up the dozen or so tubes of paint and went to the end of the counter to pack them.

"Mr. Gregg," Kendrick said, oozing charm, "I know that you are an artist. May I say that it has grieved me that after being on such excellent terms with your father, you haven't been here before."

"I am not interested in the works of other artists," Crispin said curtly. "I am only interested in my own work."

"Of course . . . of course," Kendrick smiled, now looking like a dolphin expecting a fish. "A true artist speaking." He paused, then went on. "Mr. Gregg, I would love to see some of your work. Quite recently, I was talking to Herman Lowenstein—a great art critic. He confided to me that your mother once consulted him about your work, and he was privileged to see some of it. Mr. Gregg! There are very few art critics who know their jobs. Most of them are fakes, but Lowenstein is a true judge." This was a glib lie as Kendrick regarded Lowenstein as the phoniest of all the local art critics. "He told me your work is outstanding." Again a glib lie as Lowenstein had said Crispin's work was not only unhealthy, but utterly un-commercial. "He said the vigor, the imagination, the flow of creative ideas were quite remarkable! The splendid way you use colour! Your technique! When such a great critic talks like this to me, I long to promote your work. Mr. Gregg! I can boast of running the finest art gallery on the Pacific coast! May I arrange an exhibition of your art? What a privilege! Please, don't deny me!"

Well, Kendrick thought, if this doesn't land this cold fish, nothing else will.

"My work is special," Crispin said, but he felt a tingle of excitement. He knew his mother had shown some of his landscapes to Lowenstein, but this was the first time he had heard his work had made such an impression. He suddenly felt an urge to be recognized as an artist of stature. He had many paintings, apart from his secret horror paintings. Why not? But suppose no one was interested? His work was indeed special.

Seeing him hesitating, Kendrick said, oil dripping from his voice, "You are modest, Mr. Gregg. Lowenstein can't be mistaken. Do, please, let me arrange an exhibition. Just imagine if our great modern artists had been shy. What a loss to the world!"

Still hesitating, Crispin said, "I don't think the world is ready for my work. It is too advanced. Maybe later . . . I'll think about it."

The fish is nearly hooked, Kendrick thought. He switched on his understanding smile as he said, "How well do I understand your feelings, Mr. Gregg, but give me the privilege to judge. Let me have just one painting. Let me put it in my window. I promise you I will be utterly sincere. If there is no interest—quite unthinkable!—but if there isn't I will tell you. Give me this opportunity to promote a new and vigorous artist. Let me have just one painting."

Crispin moved away while he thought. He knew his work was outstanding, but he couldn't bear the thought that these rich fools, living in Paradise City, wouldn't appreciate it, but yet. . . .

He made up his mind.

"Very well, send someone to my villa and I will give him one of my landscapes. Put it in your window, but it must be understood that the painting will be unsigned. No one is to know that I have painted it. I want the reaction of the art collectors. If they show no interest, then return the painting. If they are interested, then I will let you have more for an exhibition."

"Perfect, Mr. Gregg. I can't tell you how excited I am!"

Crispin stared at Kendrick as he said, "No one is to know who has painted this picture. It is to be the work of an unknown artist. Do you understand?" There was something in the opal coloured eyes that sent a little chill through Kendrick's fat body.

"It is utterly understood, Mr. Gregg. You can rely on me. My man will call on you this afternoon if that would be convenient."

Jo-Jo came forward, and with a flourish, presented Crispin with the box of paints.

117

"I'll have something ready for him," Crispin said, taking the box. "Bill me." Then nodding, he started down the long wide aisle that led to the gallery's exit. On either side were glass cases, artistically lit, displaying some of Kendrick's many treasures.

Crispin suddenly paused before a small show case and looked at an object, lying on white velvet.

Kendrick was on his heels.

"Ah, Mr. Gregg!" he exclaimed, his little eyes lighting up "A true artist! This unique ornament makes you pause."

Crispin was regarding the object. He had no idea why it should have attracted his attention. Some odd instinct had made him stop.

The object was some four inches long: an elegant slim block of silver, finely engraved, and with tiny rubies and emeralds made in the shape of a dagger. The object was attached to a long silver chain of filigree work.

"What is it?" Crispin asked.

"A pendant, Mr. Gregg: so fashionable these days, but much more than that. I must show you." Kendrick lifted the glass cover. Jo-Jo came forward and took the cover from Kendrick. "This is an exact replica of a pendant worn by Suleiman the Great. Suleiman went in fear of his life. This, Mr. Gregg, was his hidden protection. It is without doubt the first switch blade knife to have been invented."

Crispin's eyes narrowed.

"A switch blade knife?"

Kendrick picked the pendant from its velvet bed and laid it on his fat palm.

"Suleiman wore the original in 1540. It is reputed to have saved his life from an assassin's attack. Let Jo-Jo demonstrate. It is quite, quite fascinating." Jo-Jo came forward and Kendrick draped the silver chain around his neck and allowed the pendant to swing down, lying on Jo-Jo's narrow chest. "You see? A delightful, artistic pendant, but something very different. Jo-Jo!"

Jo-Jo pressed the top ruby on the hilt of the dagger, and

from the slab of silver, a thin, narrow-bladed knife sprang out.

"The first switch blade knife! It is utterly deadly and sharper than a razor. It is quite unique, Mr. Gregg."

Crispin stared at the glittering four inch blade. He felt a surge of sexual excitement run through him. This was something he had to possess!

"What are you asking for it?" he demanded.

This was so unexpected that Kendrick, for a split second, hesitated.

"It is quite unique, Mr. Gregg. Actually, it is a museum piece. I—"

"What do you want for it?" Crispin snapped.

"I am asking fifty thousand dollars. There is no other like it in the world, but for you, if you would like it, shall we say forty thousand?"

"Give it to me!" Crispin said to Jo-Jo who pressed the emerald at the point of the dagger and the blade snapped back. Jo-Jo hurriedly removed the chain from his neck and handed the pendant to Crispin who snatched it from him. Crispin put the chain around his neck and let the pendant drop on his chest, then he moved to a mirror and surveyed himself.

Kendrick watched. Could this be a sale? Admittedly the original pendant had been worn by Suleiman the Great. Kendrick had seen coloured drawings of it, and in an inspired moment, he had got his best silver-smith to copy it. The copy had cost three thousand dollars. The rubies and emeralds were clever fakes.

Crispin pressed the ruby and the blade sprang out.

"Pray be careful, Mr. Gregg," Kendrick said, his voice anxious. "The blade is incredibly sharp."

Crispin lifted the pendant, letting the sunlight, coming through the big window, play on the blade. Again he felt a sexual urge run through him. Then nodding to himself, he pressed the emerald button and the blade snapped out of sight.

He turned and stared at Kendrick. There was a strange

expression on his face that Kendrick couldn't define, but which made him uneasy.

"I'll take it at forty thousand," Crispin said. "Bill me," and he walked down the aisle and out onto the street, the pendant bouncing gently on his chest.

Louis, watching discretely, came forward.

"That was truly marvellous!" he gushed. "You are the most marvellous salesman!"

"There's something about that man. . . ." Kendrick began, then shrugged. He had made a thirty seven thousand dollar profit, so why should he worry about Crispin Gregg? "This afternoon, Louis, go to Mr. Gregg's place and collect one of his paintings. We will exhibit it. Although I have little confidence in Lowenstein's opinions, we have to bear in mind that he considers Mr. Gregg's work of no commercial value. Let us see for ourselves. At least, Mr. Gregg has become a client."

Then still not able to shake off his uneasiness from that strange, almost frightening expression he had seen on Crispin's face, he walked heavily back to his reception room.

*   *   *

After one hundred and seventy seven telephone calls and eighteen visits to the squad room, the citizens of Paradise City abruptly lost interest in the golf ball jacket, but they had supplied information that had to be written down and collated.

On this sunny morning at 08.00, Lepski, Jacoby and Dusty Lucas toiled at their desks.

Lepski had returned home the previous night after 01.00. He had found his living room in a shambles. His bottle of Cutty Sark stood empty on the table. There were used glasses, over-flowing ashtrays and it would seem, from the debris, Carroll had provided her guests with snacks.

He had gone up to bed to find Carroll asleep. From the soft whistling noise coming from her, he judged she was in an alcoholic stupor. Depressed by the T.V. fiasco, he had flopped into bed by her side, and finally slept. She was still sleeping when he dragged himself from the bed, showered, dressed and drove down to headquarters by 07.30.

Jacoby and Dusty joined him, and they set about reading the mass of reports the T.V. inquiry about the golf ball jacket had produced.

Finally, around 10.00, they had completed their reading and the information added up to nil. They had accurate descriptions of Ken Brandon, Harry Bentley and Sam Macree: all men seen wearing the jacket by conscientious citizens, but there was no information about the fourth jacket, once owned by the late Cyrus Gregg, and that was the information they so badly wanted.

Lepski pushed back his chair and released a snort of disgust that made both Jacoby and Dusty pause in their work.

"Not a goddam thing!" Lepski exploded. "You two got anything?"

They shook their head.

"Okay. Dusty, go talk to those two S.A. collectors. Put pressure on them. One or the other could be lying."

Lucas, an eager-beaver, nodded and took himself off.

Lepski leaned back in his chair. There was a nagging thought at the back of his mind that had nothing to do with police work. Next month would bring Carroll's birthday, and he couldn't remember the exact date. This fact had been bothering him for days. He wanted to buy her a present. He wanted to give her the present on the right day. He knew he would be in the dog-house for weeks if he didn't come up, not only with the right date, but also, with the right present. This was something he had to avoid.

Vaguely, he remembered last year, he had taken Carroll to an expensive restaurant. Maybe the Maitre d' could give him the date. Then he realized he couldn't remember the name of the restaurant. He thumped his fist on his desk with exasperation.

"Got something on your mind, Tom?" Jacoby asked,

recognizing the signs.

"Yeah. God help me, I'm trying to remember the date of Carroll's birthday."

"The day after tomorrow," Jacoby said without hesitation.

Lepski half started from his chair, his eyes bulging.

"You must be kidding! It's next month!"

"The day after tomorrow: the tenth," Jacoby said. "I keep a birthday book."

"A—what?"

"We Jewish people are sentimental," Jacoby said, smiling. "I know we are known to be mean, but we are sentimental. My father kept a birthday book. He liked to send friends a card or a present. I keep a birthday book. Carroll is a friend. I've already bought her a bottle of perfume. It will be delivered the day after tomorrow."

Lepski sucked in his breath.

"You really mean it's on the tenth?"

"That's it."

"Holy God!" Lepski's hands turned clammy. "I could have sworn it was next month! Perfume, huh? You're sending her perfume?"

"Well, I thought a wonderful girl like Carroll would like some perfume."

"Yeah . . . yeah." Lepski loosened his tie. "What the hell can I give her?"

Jacoby, who wasn't married, but had a string of girl friends, hid a grin.

"Just look around, Tom. Girls like presents."

"Yeah." Lepski stared into space. "But what the hell what?"

"A handbag. A dress. Jewels. Depends on how much you want to spend."

"It's not how much I want to spend: it's how much I can afford to spend," Lepski said. "A handbag, huh? That's an idea. Yeah. I'll give her a handbag."

A voice said, "If you two will stop yakking, can I have some attention?" A female voice, soft, sensual: a creamy voice.

Both detectives swung around and stared.

Standing at the barrier that divided the Detectives' room from the visitors was a coloured girl, and what a girl!

Both Lepski and Jacoby pointed like gun dogs, then Lepski came fast to the barrier.

The girl was the colour of coffee, gently diluted with cream. She was tall and willowy. She wore close fitting white cotton slacks and a close fitting blood red jersey top. What this outfit did to her made Lepski breath heavily through his nose. He hadn't seen a more perfect woman's body! Big, half pineapple shaped breasts, a tiny waist, a voluptuous sweep of hips, long legs. Her features were sensual: a short, thin nose with slightly flared nostrils, big black eyes that glittered with life, and full lips that suggested untold promises. Some girl!

"Yes, miss?" Lepski said, looking into the black eyes and feeling his blood move down to where it shouldn't have moved down—being a married man.

"I've come about this jacket I saw on the telly last night," the girl said. Her voice reminded Lepski of Mae West's in an old movie he had seen, murmuring "Come up and see me sometime."

He opened the gate of the barrier.

"Come on in," he said, aware that Jacoby was leaning over his desk, staring. "Have a seat."

She moved by him. Her body flowed. Her breasts did a tiny jig. Following her, Lepski watched the movement of her hips. She sat in a chair opposite Lepski's desk, opened her handbag and took from it a pack of Camels. Lepski searched through his pockets for a match, but she had already lit the cigarette with a solid gold lighter before he had found his match book.

He sat down and restrained a leer. He knew instinctively that this girl knew all the answers, and a detective, although first grade, was small fry to her, but that didn't stop him from eyeing those beautiful breasts, scarcely concealed by the jersey top.

"May I have your name, miss?" he asked and drew a scratch pad towards him.

"Doroles Hernandez. I live in apartment 165, Castle avenue. My mother got screwed by a Spanish creep who ran a factory, and I was the product. I kept his name." She gave Lepski a brilliant smile, revealing perfect white teeth. "Just the background, Mr. Detective. Do you want more?"

Lepski whistled through his nose. He knew all about Castle avenue: that was where the expensive hookers lived. So she was a hooker! Boy! He thought, if I wasn't married and five years younger, I'd be up there at apartment 165, Castle avenue, like a lizard after a fly!

"You have information, Miss Hernandez," he asked in a carefully controlled voice.

"Maybe . . . maybe not. I had a stand-up last night. The guy was sick or something," Doroles said, "so I put on the telly. I don't usually look at the telly. It's a drag, you know?"

"Yeah. So you looked at the telly and saw the jacket . . . right?" Lepski said, trying to keep his mind off those provocative breasts and on the work in hand.

"That's it." She gave him a sexy smile that almost destroyed his better feelings. "There I was all alone, with a gin martini for company. . . ." She paused and regarded him with her big, black eyes. "I bet you prefer Scotch, Mr. Detective."

Lepski, who was now wondering just how marvellous she would look without clothes, started.

"Yeah. So there you were alone and you saw the jacket?"

"Yes. As soon as I saw it, I remembered." She turned her head and caught Jacoby leaning across his desk, breathing heavily, as he gaped at her. "Is he a detective?" she asked. "He looks cute."

"His mother thought so," Lepski growled. "Let's work on this, Miss Hernandez. You saw the jacket and you remembered. What did you remember?"

"Call me Doroles." This in the Mae West voice.

Lepski was thankful the desk hid what was now happening to his lower section.

"Yeah. Well, Doroles . . . what did you remember?"

124

"I remembered seeing the jacket. I thought it was pretty sharp, you know? A real eye catcher."

"When did you see the jacket?"

"When?" She moved in the chair and her breasts did a little dance which was appreciated both by Lepski and Jacoby. "It was on the fifth."

Lepski stiffened to attention. On the evening of the fifth, Janie Bandler had been murdered.

"Are you sure about the date, Doroles? This is important."

"I'm sure. I'll tell you for why. It's Jamie's birthday. Jamie is my dog. I took him to the Blue Sky restaurant. The Maitre d' loves Jamie. Do you like dogs, Mr. Detective?"

Lepski suppressed a growling noise. He hated dogs.

"So you took your dog out. What time was this?"

"Lunch time. I'm crazy about Jamie. He's my best friend, you know? When I come home tired, he's there waiting for me. He jumps all over me. He's really sweet."

Lepski snapped the pencil he was holding.

"You were walking your dog? So what happened?"

She made a little grimace.

"Well, this guy came up to me. Guys are always coming up to me, you know?"

Lepski could imagine. If he hadn't been married, he would have gone up to her.

"And this guy was wearing the golf ball jacket?"

She stubbed out her cigarette, and immediately lit another.

"I can't stop," she said, and her sensual lips parted in a smile. "I guess I'm nervous or something. Do you think all this crap about cigarettes being dangerous is right?"

"Maybe. You were saying this guy came up to you," Lepski said. If it had been anyone but this gorgeous sex symbol, he would have been shouting by now. As it was, his face turned a dark hue.

"A cheapie."

"Was he wearing the jacket?" Lepski hissed.

Her big eyes opened wide.

"Why, no. He was wearing a sharkskin brown . . . strictly

125

for the birds."

Lepski snapped another pencil.

"We're talking about this godda . . . we're talking about this golf ball jacket."

She gave him another smile that went right down to his heels.

"You can swear if you want to, Mr. Detective. I don't mind. Lots of my men friends swear. Men do, you know?"

Lepski dug his fingers into the surface of his desk.

"So what about the jacket?"

"Well, this cheapie was chatting me up. He was offering fifty. Can you imagine?" She leaned back and laughed. She had a nice, sexy laugh, but by now, Lepski was fast losing patience. "Jamie wanted to visit a tree, then this jacket went by. As soon as I saw it, I thought it was real sharp. I like to see men well dressed. A man who cares about how he looks is the kind of man I like."

"Yeah. So you saw the jacket pass . . . who was wearing it?"

"A tall, doll of a man, you know?"

Lepski reached for his scratch pad.

"Tell me about him, Doroles. Give me a description."

She stubbed out her cigarette and lit another.

"I didn't see his face, Mr. Detective. What with this cheapie and Jamie wanting to get to a tree, you know?"

Lepski refrained from crumpling up the pad and throwing it across the room.

"Let's take this step by step," he said in a low, strangulated voice. "A man walked by, and you saw he was wearing the golf ball jacket . . . right?"

"That's absolutely correct."

"This was around lunch time of the fifth?"

She nodded.

"You didn't see this man's face, but you saw something of him?"

"Yes."

"Okay. This is important, Doroles. Was he tall, medium, short?"

126

"He was tall. I like tall men. Short men, to me, are a drag, you know?"

"So he was tall." Lepski stood up. "As tall as I am?"

She surveyed him as a butcher surveys a prime side of beef. "Even taller: not much, but taller."

Lepski sat down again.

"Was he heavily built, thin, normal, fat?"

"He had wide shoulders. I noticed that. I like men with wide shoulders, tapering away to slim hips. He had that."

"Did he wear a hat?"

"No. I liked the look of his hair: fair, you know? Really fair: call it corn and cut close. I get bored with guys with long hair."

"Doroles, you saw a man with corn coloured hair, tall, broad shouldered and around six foot tall . . . right?"

"Absolutely correct, Mr. Detective."

"What else did you notice about him?"

"He was wearing light blue slacks. They went well with the jacket, you know? And he wore Gucci shoes. I notice shoes, and I think Gucci's shoes are a real ball." She again shifted, and her breasts again did a little jig.

Lepski released a soft sigh. It wasn't fair for any detective to talk to her, he thought.

"How did he walk?"

"Well, he walked, you know? Like a man who knows where he is going . . . big strides."

"He didn't limp?"

"Oh, no."

"Doroles, this is important. This is the first lead we have to the man who killed Janie Bandler and Lu Boone. You've read about that, huh?"

"That's why I'm here. I always listen to Pete Hamilton when I'm not busy. He's a doll."

Lepski had other names to describe Hamilton, but this wasn't the time.

"We want as much information about this man you saw as you can give us. What else did you notice about him?"

She thought as she stubbed out her cigarette. She thought as she lit another.

"His hands!" She surveyed Lepski, giving him her sexy smile. "Hands mean a lot to me, Mr. Detective, you know? I have men friends, you know? Their hands . . . well, you know?"

Lepski nodded. He could well imagine a man's hands were important to a high price hooker.

"So, I noticed his hands as he passed. They were artistic: long fingers, the hands of an artist: a painter, you know?"

"He could have been a surgeon, something like that, couldn't he?"

"Maybe. He had artistic hands."

"From your description, it sounds to me as if he is in the money."

Doroles wrinkled her pretty nose.

"He could be one of these cheapies who live on expenses, you know? No money, big deal, but charging everything on credit cards for whoever he works for to pick up. There was a cheapie who actually wanted to pay me by credit card . . . can you imagine?"

"Yeah. Well, let's see if we can get something more."

"I'd like you to hurry it, Mr. Detective. I guess by now, Jamie wants to visit a tree."

But after asking more questions, Lepski decided she had nothing else of importance to tell him.

"Well, that's fine, Doroles. You've been a great help. If you saw the back of this guy, would you recognize him?"

"Sure, I would."

"Even if he wasn't wearing the jacket?"

Doroles nodded, then got to her feet. Her whole body gave a little dance. Jacoby who hadn't taken his eyes off her, caught his breath in a despairing sigh.

"One thing," Lepski said as he stood up, "say nothing to anyone about what you have told me. This is important. Up to now, you're the only one out of hundreds who has given us constructive information. This man is dangerous. If it got

128

around you could recognize him . . . you dig?"

Her big black eyes widened.

"You think he would come after me?"

"He could."

"You think he would cut me up like that poor girl?"

"He could."

"I hope you get him fast, Mr. Detective. I won't feel safe until you do."

"Just say nothing."

"Do you think I should have a bodyguard?"

Jacoby half started out of his chair, then meeting Lepski's scowl, he sat down again.

"If the Chief thinks you should have a bodyguard, I'll fix it," Lepski said.

" 'Bye for now." She flashed him a smile, flashed another to Jacoby, then flowed out of the room.

Jacoby wiped his hands on his handkerchief.

"What did she say her address was?"

"A minimum of two hundred dollars," Lepski said. "Be your age, Max. Since when has a third grade cop have two hundred bucks to spend on a hooker?" He gathered up his notes and went into Terrell's office.

*　　　*　　　*

Reynolds switched off the Pete Hamilton's ten o'clock programme and looked hesitantly at Amelia who sat in a fat heap in her chair. They had listened to the details of Lu Boone's killing. Hamilton, who liked to shock, had spared no details. He described the severed head and the horrifying mutilations of the body.

"There can be no doubt that this homicidal maniac is still in the city," he concluded. "Be on your guard. No one is safe until he is apprehended. You might well ask what the police are doing!"

"I don't believe it! I won't believe it!" Amelia exclaimed wildly. "Crispin wouldn't. . . ."

129

"I think a little brandy, madam," Reynolds said.

"Yes. . . ."

As he moved unsteadily to the liquor cabinet, through the window, he saw Crispin walk briskly to the Rolls. Crispin was on his way to the Kendrick Gallery.

"He is leaving, madam," Reynolds said as he watched the Rolls drive away.

"Go to his studio!" Amelia said. "Look!"

But first, Reynolds went to his room, poured himself a treble Scotch, swallowed it, then paused until the spirit steadied him. Then finding the length of wire to pick the lock on Crispin's apartment door, he slowly climbed the stairs.

Amelia sat and waited. She was sure that Crispin had committed another gruesome murder. She could be wrong, she told herself desperately. This time there were no blood stained clothes to get rid of. She laid a fat hand against her floppy bosom, feeling her heart thumping. He must have done it! She closed her eyes. The disgrace! Her life would come to an end! Who would want to entertain the mother of such a monster? This evening, she had been invited to join a party at the Spanish Bay hotel restaurant in honour of the French ambassador. This was her life! But who would ever invite her again to such dinners if it became known that her son was a homicidal lunatic?

She heard a sound and looked towards the door. Reynolds stood there, his face as white as cold mutton fat, sweat on his forehead. They looked at each other, then he nodded.

"What?" Amelia exclaimed, leaning forward. "Don't nod at me! What?"

"He is painting the head of a man, madam," Reynolds said, his voice a half whisper. "A severed head in blood."

Although she had been sure, what Reynolds had said was like a blow in her face. She sank back, closing her eyes.

"Brandy, Reynolds!"

He went slowly to the liquor cabinet and picked up a glass. As he reached for the cognac, the glass slipped from his shaking hand and dropped onto the carpet.

130

"Reynolds!" Amelia screamed.

"Yes, madam."

He found another glass, slopped spirit into it, then brought it to her. She seized the glass and drank.

"Madam. . . ."

"Don't talk to me. Understand, Reynolds? We know nothing! Go about your work!"

"He could continue, madam."

"Who are these people? Who cares?" Amelia's voice was shrill. "A whore! A hippy! Who cares?"

"But, madam. . . ."

"We know nothing!" Amelia screamed at him. "Do you want to lose your job? Do you imagine I want to be thrown out of my home? It is not our business! We know nothing!"

Reynolds saw the terrifying vision of himself out of work with no more unlimited supply of Scotch. He hesitated, then felt impelled to issue a warning.

"Madam, he is very dangerous. He just might attack you." He refrained from adding that Crispin might also attack him.

"Attack me? I am his mother! Stop drivelling, and go about your work! We know nothing!"

*   *   *

Terrell sat at his desk. Hess, Beigler and Lepski occupied chairs. All men were sipping coffee which Charlie Tanner had brought in.

"We are getting nearer to this mad man," Terrell said. "This is our first important break: the fourth jacket. The other three owners don't match up with this description." He looked at Lepski. "This girl satisfied you she knew what she was talking about?"

"Yeah," Lepski said. "She knew."

"So this must be the jacket Mrs. Gregg gave away to the Salvation Army. This is the jacket we want to trace." Terrell paused to light his pipe. "But according to the description of this man, he wasn't on the end of a hand-out from the S.A. A man who can afford Gucci shoes could afford to buy his own jacket . . . right?"

"We have a load of phonies living here," Hess said. "Guys who haven't a dime. Gigolos, stags, con men: you name them, we have them, all battening on the rich, trying for the fast buck, and these guys have to keep up an appearance. Could be this guy spotted the jacket on the S.A. truck and either stole it or offered a five spot for it. Maybe he got his Gucci shoes either by stealing them or from a clothes dealer at a knock down price."

Terrell nodded.

"Could be. So okay, let's check the clothes dealers. Tom, you get it organized. We want to know if any dealer has sold a pair of Gucci shoes and to whom."

At this moment Dusty Lucas came in.

"Chief, I think I've got something," he said excitedly. "I've been checking on those two S.A. collectors. I've got the truck driver here—Joe Heinie. His father is Syd Heinie who runs a used clothes store in Secomb. I went to this guy's home and caught him unloading a bundle of clothes off the S.A. truck. He's admitted he passes some of the clothes they collect to his father to sell."

Hess got to his feet.

"I'll handle him, Chief."

Joe Heinie was sitting on a bench the other side of the barrier with a patrolman standing over him. He was around twenty eight, tall, thin with a mop of dirty black hair and a sullen expression on his badly shaven face.

Hess and Lepski sat him down in front of a desk, then with Lepski hovering near him, Hess sat down, facing him.

"You could be in trouble, Joe," Hess said.

Heinie looked up and sneered.

"Trouble? You're crazy! What trouble? These goddam clothes are given away . . . right?"

"They are given to the Salvation Army. You have no right to take them for yourself," Hess snapped.

"Yeah? What does the S.A. do with them? They give them

132

away. So what's wrong in giving a few to my father? What's the difference?

"How long have you been doing this?"

"Six months . . . I don't remember. Who cares?"

"You'll care, Joe. You have been stealing clothes from the Salvation Army. Could get you three months."

Heinie sneered again.

"Yeah? You can't pin a charge on me. I know my rights. Some fink gives me clothes. He *gives* them to me . . . right? Okay, so I pick out a few items and give them to my father . . . right? Then I give the rest to the S.A." He leaned forward and jabbing his finger in Hess's direction, he went on, "The clothes are not the S.A.'s property until I deliver them . . . right?"

"The clothes are the property of the S.A. the moment you put them in the S.A.'s truck," Hess said, looking smug.·

Heinie's sneer deepened.

"That's right," he said, "but the goddam truck is mine! I help the S.A. voluntarily. I pay for the gas and the insurance. So, I'm entitled to give my old man some clothes to pay my expenses . . . right?"

Hess breathed heavily.

"Never mind," he said, realizing he wasn't going to get anywhere with Heinie. "We are interested in this blue jacket with golf ball buttons. Did you give such a jacket to your father?"

"How should I know?" Heinie demanded. "I don't examine everything I give my old man. I give him a bundle, and he picks what he can sell, then gives the rest back to me, and I give them to the S.A."

Hess looked at Lepski.

"Check with his father," he said.

As Lepski left, he heard Heinie say, "So I'm not in trouble, huh? I can't afford the time to sit around chewing the fat with you. . . ."

"A real smart ass," Lepski thought as he hurried to his car. He drove fast to Secomb.

133

Syd Heinie was tall like his son, with hard little eyes and a rat-trap of a mouth. His store was crammed with discarded clothing. When Lepski strode in, Heinie was measuring a fat black for a pair of trousers.

Lepski moved restlessly around until the purchase was made, then Heinie came to him. He surveyed Lepski, and instinctively knew he was a cop. He smiled, but his eyes hardened.

Lepski flashed his shield, and in his cop voice, said, "We are looking for a blue jacket with white golf ball buttons. Have you had such a jacket through your hands?"

Heinie put the stub of a pencil in his right ear, twisted it, removed it and flicked off a piece of wax.

"I can't say I have," he said. "With white golf ball buttons?"

Lepski restrained his impatience with an effort.

"Yeah."

Heinie dug the pencil stud into his left ear, twisted it, removed it and flicked more wax.

"Golf ball buttons, huh? Let me think." He rubbed the back of his neck. "Unusual kind of jacket, huh?"

Lepski made a soft growling noise.

"Well, now I think of it, I did have a jacket with golf ball buttons."

Lepski stiffened to attention. At last, a break!

"You said blue, didn't you?" Heinie asked.

"Yeah."

Heinie shook his head.

"This jacket was brown. I remember it. Must have been two years, maybe three years ago. Sort of jacket that sticks in the mind, huh?"

"This jacket is blue!" Lepski snarled.

Heinie thought some more.

"No . . . I haven't seen it."

"Look, Mr. Heinie, this is important," Lepski rasped. "This is to do with a murder investigation."

"Sure . . . sure." Heinie nodded. "No, I haven't seen a blue jacket with golf ball buttons. A brown one . . . sure, back two, three years ago, but no blue one."

"Maybe one of your staff. . . ."

"I don't have a staff," Heinie said. "Who wants staff these days?"

Police work! Lepski thought in disgust. "Gucci shoes?"

"Huh?"

"Have you sold a pair of Gucci shoes to anyone anytime?"

"You mean those Italian shoes?"

"Yeah."

"Don't ever get them. You want a fine pair of shoes? I can show you. . . ."

"Forget it!" Lepski snarled. "And watch it, Heinie! Your son could get into trouble giving you clothes intended for the Salvation Army."

"Not Joe . . . he's too smart to get into trouble," Heinie said, and grinned.

Lepski stamped out of the store and made his way to his car. Then the thought struck him he had to buy a handbag for Carroll. He paused by his car. Where the hell was he going to buy a goddam handbag on Saturday afternoon? If there was one thing Lepski loathed it was shopping.

"Hi, Mr. Lepski!"

Turning, Lepski found Karen Sternwood at his side. His eyes ran over her: some doll, he thought.

"Hi, there, Miss Sternwood. How are you doing?"

She pouted.

"I am just grabbing a hamburger. Imagine! My boss has gone off for the week-end and left me a raft of work. I'll be working all afternoon. Saturday! Imagine!"

"Mr. Brandon away?"

"His father-in-law's sick. He won't be back until Monday. How's the murder investigation going?"

"We're working at it." Lepski had a sudden idea. "Miss Sternwood, you could help me if you would have the time."

Her eyelashes fluttered. Sweet Pete! Lepski thought, if this babe hasn't hot pants then I'm a monkey's uncle.

"For you, I have time," she said.

Lepski eased his shirt collar.

"I have to buy my wife a handbag for her birthday. How do I go about it?"

"That's no problem. What kind of handbag?"

"I wouldn't know. Something fancy, I guess. My wife is pretty choosey."

Karen laughed.

"Most women are. The point is how much do you want to spend? Five hundred dollars? Something like that?"

"Well, not that high. I thought around a hundred."

"You can't do better than try Lucille's boutique on Paradise avenue," Karen said. "You can rely on her." She smiled, fluttered her eye lashes, thrust her breasts at him as she went on, "I've got to get this hamburger. See you," and she walked away, swishing her hips while Lepski stared after her.

Getting in his car, he drove fast to Paradise avenue. The luxury shops kept open on Saturday afternoon, and the side walks were crowded with people, shop window gazing. Parking his car, Lepski set off down the long avenue, looking for Lucille's boutique. He had got half-way down the avenue, cursing to himself, when he passed Kendrick's gallery. It was only because he was looking desperately at every passing shop window that he saw Crispin's landscape in Kendrick's window.

He came to an abrupt halt as he stared at the painting, then he felt the hairs on the back of his neck bristle.

A red blood moon!

A black sky!

An orange beach!

He stepped up to the window and again stared at the painting.

"Holy Pete!" he thought. "That old rum-dum's prophecy!"

He remembered she had been right when he had been hunting that killer last year. She had said he was to look for oranges, and the killer had been selling oranges!

Could she be right again?

Then he remembered what Doroles had said: *the hands of an artist.*

Could the man who had painted this landscape be the killer they were hunting for?

He hesitated for a long moment, then walked purposely into the gallery.

seven

LOUIS DE MARNEY was sulking. He considered Kendrick's insistence to keep the gallery open on Saturday afternoon a drag. He also considered that Kendrick's insistence that he, as head salesman, should remain, while the rest of the boys enjoyed themselves in their various ways, utterly unfair. Admittedly, some eight weeks ago, some doddery old cow had wandered in and bought a Holbein minature (a brilliant fake) for sixty thousand dollars. Since then, no one had visited the gallery on Saturday afternoon, but Kendrick was optimistic.

"You never know, cheri," he said to Louis, "the door may open and some sucker come in. After all, you have Sundays and Thursdays: what more can you expect?"

Apart from sulking, Louis was outraged that he had to drive to the Gregg villa and to receive a wrapped canvas from an obviously drunken butler. On removing the wrapping, back at the gallery, he found himself confronted by one of Crispin's landscapes.

"We can't show this!" he shrilled. "Look at it!"

In dismay, Kendrick studied the landscape.

"Very advanced," he said, and took off his wig to wipe his dome with a silk hankerchief.

"Advanced?" Louis shrilled. "It's an insult to art!"

"Put it in the window, cheri," Kendrick said. "You never know."

"But I do know!" Louis screamed. "It will lower the tone of our lovely gallery!"

"Control yourself, Louis!" Kendrick snapped. "Put it in

the window! I said I would show it, and I have to show it." He tapped Louis gently on his shoulder. "Remember, cheri, he owes us forty thousand dollars. Put it in the side window by itself," then shaking his head, he returned to his reception room.

Louis cleared the side window and put Crispin's painting on an easel and in the window. Then he flounced to his desk and sat down, seething with fury.

He was trying to divert his mind with a gay magazine when Lepski entered the gallery.

Louis looked up and stiffened. He knew by sight and name every cop in the city, and he knew Lepski was a renowned trouble maker. He edged his foot to a concealed button under the carpet and pressed it. Kendrick, who was going through an illustrated art book, looking for something he could fake, saw the red light gleam on his desk and knew at once that he was about to have a visit from the police. This didn't bother him. There were no hot objects d'art in the gallery, but he was surprised. The police hadn't visited his gallery for the past six months. He heaved himself out of his chair, went to the Venetian mirror, set his wig askew and then, moving like a cat, he opened his door a crack to listen.

Louis had risen from his chair. His rat-like face was wreathed in smiles.

"Detective Lepski!" he gushed. "Such a stranger! Let me guess! You are looking for a gift for your beautiful wife! An anniversary! A birthday! A special occasion! How right you are to come to us! I have the very thing! Detective Lepski! For you, we can make a very special price! Let me show you!"

Somewhat dazed by this reception, Lepski hesitated. Louis swished by him, opened a glass covered case and produced a brooch set with lapis lazuli stones.

"How your wife would love this, Detective Lepski!" Louis said excitedly. "Regard it! An Italian antique of the sixteenth century! How her friends would envy her! It's unique. To anyone else, I wouldn't sell it under one thousand dollars! But for you: five hundred! Think of the joy it would give her!"

139

Lepski pulled himself together. He gave Louis his cop stare. "That picture in the window: the one with the red moon."

Louis started and gaped, then quickly recovered himself.

"How wise! How perceptive! Of course. Such a striking painting on your wall would constantly remind your beautiful wife of you!"

"I don't want to buy it," Lepski snarled, his temper rising. "I want to know who painted it."

"You don't want to buy it?" Louis said in faked amazement.

"I want to know who painted it!"

Kendrick decided it was time for him to appear on the scene. He walked heavily into the gallery, looking a complete freak with his wig askew.

"It can't be!" he exclaimed. "Surely, you are Detective 1st Grade Lepski." He advanced. "Welcome to my modest gallery. You are inquiring aboobout the painting in our window?"

"I'm asking who painted it!" Lepski snapped.

"Who painted it?" Kendrick raised his eyebrows. "You are interested in modern art? How wise! You buy a painting today, and in a few years, you treble your outlay."

Lepski made a noise like a fall of gravel.

"This is police business. Who painted it?"

To give Kendrick time, Louis said, "He is referring to the painting with the red moon, cheri."

Kendrick nodded, lifted his wig and set it further askew on his head.

"Of course. Who painted it? Ah! Now you have raised a problem, Detective Lepski. I don't know."

"What do you mean—you don't know?"

"If I remember rightly an artist left it with us to sell. Although the painting has certain talent, it has no great value. I thought it would be fun to put it in the window over the week-end. Saturday afternoons are good for the young trade. I would let it go for fifty dollars. It would be cheerful in a youngster's room, don't you think?"

"Who was the artist?" Lepski rasped.

Kendrick heaved a regretful sigh.

"To the best of my knowledge he didn't leave a name nor did he sign the painting. He said he would call back, but so far he hasn't."

"When did he leave the painting with you?"

"A few weeks ago. Time goes by so quickly. Do you remember, cheri?" Kendrick smiled at Louis.

"No." Louis shrugged indifferently.

"What was this artist like? I want a description," Lepski said.

"What was he like?" Kendrick looked sad. "I didn't deal with him. Do you remember, Louis?"

"I didn't deal with him either," Louis said with another indifferent shrug.

Lepski eyed the two and felt instinctively they were lying.

"Then who saw him?"

"One of my staff. Artists continually come in here with paintings. Sometimes, we take the painting. These paintings are put in our cellar and from time to time, I look at them, and select something for the window. I don't know who actually dealt with this artist."

"This is police business," Lepski said. "We have reason to believe the man who painted this picture is connected with the killing of Janie Bandler and Lu Boone. I don't have to tell you about them, do I?"

Kendrick felt his heart miss a beat, but he was a master at controlling his expressions. He merely lifted his eyebrows.

"What makes you think that?"

"Never mind that! I want a description of this man! He could be the homicidal killer."

Kendrick thought of Crispin Gregg. He also remembered that Crispin owed him forty thousand dollars.

"I will ask my staff, Detective Lepski. They are not here on Saturday. You understand? Young people must have a little time off from the chores of daily work. One of them could remember."

Lepski shifted from one foot to the other. He was almost sure he was being conned.

"I'll spell it out," he said. "We are looking for a man with fair hair, around six foot tall, with artistic hands. Last seen, he was wearing a blue jacket with white golf ball buttons, pale blue slacks and Gucci shoes. We have reason to believe this man is responsible for two savage, mad murders. He could strike again any time. Now, I'm asking you for the last time, do you know the man who painted that picture?"

Kendrick felt a trickle of cold sweat run down his fat back. Just for a moment, he flinched, and Lepski saw the flinch.

There was a pause while Kendrick's quick silver mind went into action. There had been something frightening in Crispin Gregg's expression that even now haunted him. Could he be this killer? Suppose he was? Suppose he (Kendrick) gave information that led to his arrest? Forty thousand dollars gone phut! The Suleiman pendant could never be re-sold!

"I had no idea how serious this is," he said, shaking his head. "Detective Lepski! You can rely on me. On Monday, when my staff is here, I will ask them. But better, Detective Lepski, if you would come here on Monday morning, you could ask them yourself."

"Where is your staff?" Lepski snarled.

"Ah! That I don't know. I have five clever young men working for me. They could be out of town . . . they could be anywhere. The week-ends are their own. But on Monday, they will all be here."

"Now listen," Lepski snarled in his cop voice, "anyone shielding this killer becomes an accessory to two murders. Remember that! I'll be here Monday morning," and he stamped out of the gallery.

When Kendrick saw Lepski disappear, he turned to Louis.

"Don't involve me!" Louis shrilled. "Why didn't you tell him? An accessory to two murders!"

"Tell him?" Kendrick tore off his wig and threw it across the gallery. "Gregg owes me forty thousand dollars!"

"Don't involve me!" Louis repeated. "I have had enough!

I'm going for a swim! You must take all responsibility!'' and he flounced out of the gallery.

*   *   *

Karen Sternwood finally cleared her desk. The mail had been heavy and business brisk. Without Ken to help out, her Saturday afternoon had been completely taken up with routine work. She looked at her watch. The time was 18.30.

She thought of her father with a bunch of oldies on his yacht. He had invited her, but she had said she had to work and her father had been impressed. She had explained Ken had to go to his father-in-law who was very sick and she had to hold the fort. Her father had approved.

Now the work was finished, the desk cleared, and she pushed back her chair, lit a cigarette, and contemplated what was left of her week-end.

She felt horny.

She hadn't had a man since Ken, and she now felt like having a man. It was a complete drag that she couldn't drive until her licence had been restored. She decided she would spend the rest of the week-end in her cabin, but first, to find a man.

She thought of her various men friends. The trouble there, she thought, was they would be already booked. Her men friends were always careful not to have a vacant week-end.

She grimaced, then a thought struck her. Why not experiment? Why not thumb a ride and see what happened? Some interesting man might come along. Why not? It could be fun!

She locked the office and walked up Seaview avenue to the Miami highway. She stood under the shade of a palm tree, watching the passing cars. They moved slowly in the Saturday evening jam.

A Porsche approached, but it was driven by a fat, dreary looking man and she let that one go, although the driver looked inquiringly and hopefully at her. She disliked fat men.

143

The stream of Fords, Mercedes, VWs and Cadillacs crept by, but the drivers, some of them of interest to her, had a girl at their sides. She was beginning to lose patience when she saw a Rolls approaching. At this moment there was a traffic block, and the Rolls came to a standstill right by her. After regarding the driver, she didn't hesitate. He was blond, handsome and much more important, on his own. Moving up to the car, she gave the driver a dazzling, sexy smile.

"Going my way?" she asked.

Crispin Gregg regarded her. His first thought was that she would make a wonderful subject for a painting. Then he saw the blatant sexual invitation in her eyes. He leaned over and opened the off-side door.

"Where is your way?" he asked, as Karen slid into the passenger's seat.

"Paddler's Creek." She smiled at him. "What a dream of a car!"

The traffic began to move.

"Paddler's Creek?" Crispin said as he moved the car forward. "That's the Hippy colony."

"That's right."

"But you're no hippy."

She laughed and thrust out her breasts.

"I have a cabin near the colony. I am Karen Sternwood."

"Sternwood?" Crispin looked sharply at her. "There is a Sternwood to do with insurance who was friendly with my father."

"His daughter. Your father? Who are you?"

"Crispin Gregg, my father was Cyrus Gregg. He died a few months ago."

"You are his son? I once met your father. I liked him. How odd!"

"Yes." Crispin took one hand off the driving wheel and fingered the Suleiman pendant. Since he had had it, he found the urge to keep fingering it.

"That's original," Karen said, seeing the pendant in his fingers. "What it is?"

"Something I picked up," Crispin's eyes shifted. "I have something to do. It won't take a few minutes. Are you in a hurry?"

Karen laughed.

"I have all the time in the world! I am at a loose end this week-end. I have nothing to do."

Crispin nodded.

"That makes two of us. Perhaps we might do something together?"

Looking at his lean body, his long legs, his artistic hands and his handsome face, Karen felt a rush of hot blood move down to her loins.

"Yes, you wonderful man!" she thought. "We will certainly do something together!"

"That would be fun," she said.

Crispin swung the Rolls off the highway and down Paradise avenue.

"There is something I want to see, then my time is yours."

At this hour of 19.10, Paradise avenue was deserted. All the luxury shops had now closed. Crispin pulled up outside Kendrick's gallery.

Since he had parted with his landscape, he had itched to see it displayed in this renowned gallery. He wondered if there had already been inquiries. Saturday afternoon, of course, was a bad time, but he wanted to see how this stupid looking queer has displayed his painting.

There it was! On a silver painted easel! The last rays of the sun fell directly on it.

Crispin felt a surge of pride run through him. Yes! It was original! It had life!

"What do you think of that?" he asked, and pointed to the painting.

Karen stared, frowned, stared again, then looked at him.

"That thing there?"

Crispin's smile became fixed.

"That painting."

Karen shrugged.

145

"I don't know much about modern art. I have a few interesting works. My father has some of the great modern paintings."

Crispin's long artistic fingers tightened on the steering wheel.

"What do you think of that painting in the window." he said, an edge to his voice.

"It must be a joke . . . a week-end joke," Karen said. "Either that or Kendrick has gone out of his tiny mind. That? Why it looks to me as if an idiot child painted it. Don't you agree?"

"An idiot child?" Crispin said.

She laughed.

"Or a mad man. What a thing!"

Crispin's fingers caressed the Suleiman pendant.

"I thought it was original."

"Is that all you want to see?" Karen asked. She was now impatient to get this hunk of a man to her cabin. "Let's go."

Crispin shifted into "drive" and headed back to the highway.

"Seriously, if you are interested in good modern art," Karen said, "not utter junk like that, you should talk to Kendrick. He really knows."

"Utter junk?" Crispin said. "You really think that?"

"Well, don't you?"

Crispin felt a vicious urge to pull up, press the ruby stone, then stab this girl and keep on stabbing her, but he managed to control the urge.

"So you are free for the week-end," he said, his voice deceptively mild. "What would you like us to do?"

"Let's go to my cabin. You'll like it." She gave him a sexy smile. "We'll have fun."

Neither of them said anything during the short drive.

"Leave the car here," Karen said. "It's only a short walk."

Crispin drove the Rolls under the shadow of a palm tree, and together they walked down the path towards Karen's cabin.

146

Crispin said, "Isn't it around here that girl got killed?" Knowing, of course, it was.

"Yes. Wasn't that terrible?"

Dusk was falling, and the path, over-hung by trees and boxed in by shrubs, was almost dark.

Crispin moved closer.

"Aren't you scared to use this path?" and he fingered the Suleiman pendant.

"Not with a he-man like you with me."

They came out into the open.

"There it is! All mine!" Karen said and pointed.

Crispin regarded the lonely cabin.

"Looks good. You stay there quite alone? Don't the hippies bother you?"

"They dig me." Karen unlocked the door. "I dig them."

They entered the cabin and Karen turned on the lights. She crossed to the big window and drew the curtains.

Crispin looked around, nodding his approval.

"Very nice," he said.

"I love it!" Karen regarded him. Some man! she thought. "How about a drink?"

Crispin went up to her. He put his hands gently on her arms, then turned her, so her back was to him. Then very lightly, he ran his fingers down her spine.

Karen shuddered, hunched her shoulders, feeling a wave of sexual excitement run through her.

"Do it again!" she said. "How did you guess?"

Again his fingers moved from the nape of her neck down to the end of her spine.

"I love it!"

He pushed her gently towards the bed.

"Wait!" Karen slipped out of her T shirt, dropped her jeans, whipped down her panties. Then she fell face down across the bed.

"Do it!" she said breathlessly. "Again and again!"

Crispin sat on the bed by her side. He moved a finger of his left hand down her naked back. With his right hand, he lifted

147

the Suleiman pendant from his neck. His finger pressed the ruby, and the blade sprang out.

"I love it!" Karen moaned. "More!"

What felt like a feather moved down her spine. The razor sharp blade gently parted her skin and blood began to well out. There was no pain: just sexual ecstasy to her. Again the knife parted her skin in a second long line from her nape to the end of her spine. More blood began to well out.

"God!" Kared gasped, thumping her clenched fists on the bed. "This is marvellous! Do it again!"

Crispin's eyes suddenly lit up, and his lips turned into a snarl. He cut deeper, and made a long, terrible gash down the length of her body. Blood began to pour onto the sheet. Feeling sharp pain, Karen stiffened, then whirled around onto her back. She stared with horror at Crispin's face: the face of a savage, terrifying demon. She saw the blood stained blade.

"What are you doing?" she cried, her voice shrill. "What have you done to me?"

Then she saw the blood on the sheet, and as her mouth formed into a big O to scream, Crispin struck.

*　　　*　　　*

The sales girl at Lucille's Boutique wore a claret coloured trouser suit and she had a fringe hair-do. With a welcoming smile, she drifted towards Lepski as he entered the shop.

"Can I help you?" she asked, and Lepski was aware she was looking him over, judging what he was worth.

"I want a handbag," he said. "Around a hundred bucks."

She surveyed him again with her deep blue eyes.

"A present?" Her eyebrows lifted. "A hundred?"

Lepski shifted from one foot to the other. This wasn't his scene, but as he had come this far, he had to get the goddamn bag.

"A present for my wife."

"I have just the thing: a baby mink crocodile. Your wife will adore it." The bag was laid on the counter. "It has everything: chamois leather lined. Matching lipstick and compact . . . purse. . . ."

Lepski regarded the bag. He knew at once that Carroll would flip her lid to have a bag like this. What he didn't realize was that Carroll would want a new dress, a new coat, new gloves and new shoes to go with the bag.

"Yeah. Very nice. How much?"

"Two hundred and fifty." The girl smiled at him. "It is a beautiful bag. Any lady would be proud to own it."

Lepski had one hundred and ninety five dollars in his billfold. He looked at the bag regretfully.

"Too much," he said firmly. "I want something around a hundred and fifty . . . not more."

"There's this antelope, but, of course, it's not in the same class."

Another bag was produced. Lepski scarcely looked at it as he continued to eye the crocodile bag.

"Will you take my check?" he asked.

"Do we know you?" the girl asked, her smile fading.

Lepski produced his shield.

"Detective Lepski. City police."

The girl's reaction startled him. Her eyes opened wide and she positively beamed at him.

"Mr. Lepski? I can give you a discount. Suppose we say a hundred and seventy?"

Lepski gaped at her.

"My brother works at headquarters: Dusty Lucas," the girl went on. "He's often talked about you. He says you are the smartest cop on the force."

Lepski preened himself.

"We have a deal, and let me tell you, Miss Lucas, your brother is no slouch either."

She gift wrapped the bag while Lepski counted out his money.

"I appreciate this, Miss Lucas," he went on. He gave her his wolf leer. "Dusty is lucky to have a sister as gorgeous as you."

"Why, Mr. Lepski! That's quite a compliment. You tell him."

Lepski nodded.

"Yeah. Brothers don't appreciate sisters, but I'll tell him."

Out on the street, he looked at his watch. The time was 18.45. There was no point in checking out any more clothes dealers. By now, they would have closed shop. He got in his car, lit a cigarette, and thought. He found himself in a quandary. This old rum-dum, Mehitabel Bessinger, had said he would find the killer by the clues of a blood red moon, a black sky and an orange beach. She had been right the previous time when she said he would find the killer he had been hunting among oranges. Lepski hated to admit it, but it looked as if this old-rum knew what she was talking about. He should have realized right away that she had been talking about a painting. It had been sheer chance that he had seen this painting in Kendrick's window. He knew Kendrick was a fence. He felt sure he had been lying when he had said he didn't know who the artist who had painted the picture. He was sure that Kendrick was covering for someone. Lepski shoved his hat to the back of his head while he thought. He knew for sure that Kendrick would never cover anyone unless this someone was rich.

Lepski tossed his cigarette out of the car window. He couldn't tell his Chief about Mehitabel Bessinger. The thought of explaining to Terrell that Carroll had consulted a drunken clairvoyant, and this rum-dum had given out these clues, brought Lepski out in a cold sweat. Terrell, and the rest of the boys, would laugh themselves sick. They would think he had gone crazy. No, this was something he had to follow up himself: saying nothing. On Monday he would go to Kendrick's gallery and take Kendrick's staff apart.

He drove back to headquarters. After typing his report about his talk with Syd Heinie, he took it to Terrell.

After reading the report, Terrell shrugged. "Okay, Tom. Go home. Sooner or later, we'll get a break."

Lepski got home at 23.15. As usual, he found Carroll glued

to the goggle box. She waved to him. The gangster movie was exciting. She couldn't take her eyes off the lighted screen.

"There's food in the refrig."

T.V.! Lepski thought sourly. A goddam drug!

He ate cold chicken and drank beer in the kitchen. As he listened to the sound of gunfire, police sirens and strident voices coming from the T.V., he helped himself to more beer.

At midnight, the film finished, and he walked into the living room. Carroll, her mind now switched off from the gangster violence, smiled at him.

"A good day?" she asked.

"Right now, it is your birthday," Lepski said smugly. "A present!"

"Oh, Tom! I was sure you would forget!"

"That's a nice thing to say." He placed the gift wrapped bag on her lap. "First grade detectives never forget!"

When she saw the handbag, she gave a squeal of delight.

At 02.30, Lepski was woken by the shrill sound of the telephone bell. Cursing, he rolled out of bed and stumbled into the living room, grabbing the telephone receiver.

"Tom?" Beigler barked. "Get down here fast! This sonofabitch has killed again. Guess who? Sternwood's daughter," and he hung up.

*   *   *

Amelia Gregg came slowly awake from a drugged sleep. She looked around her familiar luxury bedroom with relief. She had had a spine chilling dream. She kept dreaming that she was walking through the big lounge of the Spanish Bay hotel. All her friends were sitting in the lounge, but when they saw her, they turned away. They began to whisper together. The whispers reached Amelia as she plodded across the deep pile of the carpet.

Her son is mad. He is a monster. He is mad . . . mad . . . mad.
The whispering voices built up into a strident sound that hammered inside her head.

151

Mad . . . mad . . . mad!

In her dream, she stumbled forward, hiding her face in her hands, then as if the film had been reversed, she found herself once more entering the lounge, but the voices were now deafening.

Mad . . . mad . . . mad!

She had woken, shuddering. She looked at the bedside clock. The time was 02.30. Dragging her bulk from the bed, she had gone to the bathroom and had taken two Valium pills.

Now she was awake again. It was 09.45. What a dream! No one must know! This dreadful dream had been the writing on the wall! She knew she would have no friends, no future life, if Crispin was discovered.

She pressed the bell push on her bedside table to alert Reynolds that she would be getting up. She needed strong black coffee. When she came into the living room, Reynolds was pouring coffee with an unsteady hand. She regarded him sharply, and she saw at once he was drunk.

"Reynolds! You drink too much!" she snapped as she sat down.

"Yes, madam," Reynolds said. "Will you need breakfast?"

"No. where is he?"

"In his apartment, madam."

"He went out last night?"

"Yes, madam."

"Did you hear him return?"

"Just after ten o'clock, madam."

Amelia sipped the coffee gratefully.

"Put on the television, Reynolds. Pete Hamilton."

"Yes, madam."

First, came Pete Hamilton with the background scene of Karen Sternwood's cabin with police officers milling around, then a still shot of Karen, then the words that turned Amelia to stone.

The maniac killer had struck again. Karen Sternwood, the daughter of the multi-millionaire, had been brutally murdered and mutilated.

"This is the third time this madman has killed in less than a week," Hamilton went on.."The police are certain someone is sheltering him. Mr. Jefferson Sternwood is now offering a reward." On the screen came a still of Sternwood: a cruel granite-hard face that made Amelia's heart accelerate. "Mr. Sternwood is offering two hundred thousand dollars to anyone who gives information that will lead to the arrest of this madman." Hamilton paused. "Two hundred thousand dollars!" he repeated. "Information received will be treated in strict confidence. Anyone who can give definite proof who this killer is has only to telephone police headquarters, and he or she will be paid two hundred thousand dollars, and no questions asked." Hamilton then switched to other local news.

There was silence in the room as Reynolds turned off the T.V. set.

Two hundred thousand dollars! Amelia thought. Even for a million dollars she wouldn't sacrifice her social life!

Two hundred thousand dollars! Reynolds was thinking. Freedom! No more chores! No more waiting on this fat old woman! All he had to do was to telephone the police. Then, with two hundred thousand dollars, he would buy a little villa and a piece of land and settle in peace for the rest of his days with all the Scotch he could ever hope to drink!

Then he became aware that Amelia was staring at him.

"Reynolds!" she said, half suspecting that he was contemplating treachery. "We must say nothing! Money isn't everything! Think of me! My life would be ruined! I rely on your loyalty."

His face expressionless, Reynolds bowed. What a vain old fool! he thought. Did she really imagine he would keep silent now such a reward was being offered?

"Yes, madam," he said "Perhaps another cup of coffee?"

"No. I will talk to Mr. Crispin. We must pay you more, Reynolds," Amelia said desperately. "Be loyal to me, and I promise you you won't regret it."

153

"You may rely on me, madam. I have served you so long."
Reynold's voice was wooden. "A little more coffee, madam?"

"No . . . no."

"Then I will remove the tray."

Could she trust him? Amelia wondered, watching him as he
picked up the tray and moved towards the door.

"Reynolds!"

He paused.

"Yes, madam."

"What are you doing today?"

"I have your lunch to prepare, then as it is Sunday, and as
it is so fine, perhaps a walk."

"I am not feeling well. This has been a great shock. Would
you be kind and stay? I don't want to be left alone."

"Certainly, madam. As you know, I am always at your
disposal."

With a little bow, he left her.

On the other side of the city, Claude Kendrick turned off
the T. V. set.

Kendrick was sitting in his luxury living room in his
apartment above the gallery, having finished breakfast. He
was an expert cook and he believed, on Sundays, he should
cook himself something special, then do without lunch, and go
out to dinner. He had grilled two baby lamb chops, four
lamb's kidneys which he had placed on a bed of tiny peas.
Strong black coffee, toast and marmalade completed the
meal, but Pete Hamilton's broadcast had given him
indigestion.

Two hundred thousand dollars!

He considered the possibility of claiming the reward, but
regretfully decided that he had no real proof that Crispin
Gregg was the killer. What baffled him was why Lepski had
said that Gregg's painting was connected with the killer. Why
had he said that? Admittedly, Lepski's description of the
wanted man fitted Gregg, but there were thousands of tall,
blond men around. Kendrick thumped his chest, trying to
ease his heartburn. Just suppose Gregg could prove he had

154

nothing to do with the killings? Just suppose it leaked that he (Kendrick) had informed? So many of his clients relied on him when dealing with stolen property to keep silent. Once an informer, always an informer. No, in spite of the size of the reward, in the long run, it would be more advantageous to say nothing. Then he thought of Louis de Marney. Would Louis want the reward? A silly question! Of course he would! Lumbering to his feet, Kendrick telephoned Louis who had a three room apartment within five minutes walk of the gallery.

His voice thick with sleep, Louis answered the call.

"Come at once, cheri!" Kendrick barked. "I must talk to you, and do nothing until we have talked!"

"Do nothing about what?" Louis shrilled. "This is Sunday!"

Kendrick realized that Louis hadn't seen the Hamilton programme. He visualized Louis in bed with some boy.

"Never mind! Come as soon as you can," and he hung up.

Crispin Gregg turned off his T.V. set. Two hundred thousand dollars! His eyes narrowed. He had made a dangerous mistake killing that disgusting little whore.

Who knew? Only his mother and Reynolds. His mother? Her social position meant everything to her. Reynolds? Yes, Reynolds would betray him. Reynolds, with his drink problem, wouldn't hesitate to claim the reward.

Crispin sat for some moments, fingering the Suleiman pendant, then he got to his feet. Moving in cat-like silence, he left his apartment and stood at the head of the stairs. He listened. He could hear Reynolds washing up in the kitchen. Silently, he ran down the stairs and to Reynolds' room. He opened the door and moved into the neat bed-sitting room. The smell of whisky made him grimace. He looked around. The window, over-looking the garden, had iron bars. Because the living quarters were on ground level, Amelia had insisted that every window should have bars.

He saw the extension telephone. He pressed the ruby button, and with the razor sharp blade, he cut the telephone cord. Then he moved to the door, took the key from the lock

155

and moved out into the corridor, closing the door.

Half-way down the corridor was a walk-in broom closet. He stepped inside, leaving the door ajar.

Chrissy, the deaf-mute cook, had watched the Pete Hamilton broadcast. She knew nothing about the murders Hamilton was talking about. She took no interest in local news, but she was impressed when she learned there was a two hundred thousand dollar reward. What could she do with money like that! Sunday was her day off. She had gone to Mass at 07.00 and now, she intended to watch T.V. Knowing Reynolds' habits, she was waiting until he had left the kitchen. She wanted to get the remains of a chicken pie she had left in the refrigerator for her lunch. Still thinking how wonderful it would be to own two hundred thousand dollars, she opened her door, then hastily stepped back into her room.

She watched through the crack in the door as Crispin removed the key from Reynolds' lock. She watched him step into the broom closet.

A few minutes later, Reynolds left the kitchen, came down the corridor, entered his room and closed the door.

Watched by Chrissy, a puzzled expression on her face, Crispin left the broom closet and gently inserted the key into the lock of Reynolds' door, turned it, removed it and dropped it into his pocket. She watched him walk down the corridor to his mother's living room.

Reynolds poured himself a large scotch and sat down. Two hundred thousand dollars! He would call the police! He had all the proof they needed! Those gruesome paintings on the walls! The ashes of the blood stained clothes he had burned! He was sure the police would find some clues among the ashes. He had peered into the furnace and seen, although charred, the golf ball buttons hadn't been destroyed. What was he waiting for? Tell them now! Hamilton had said all information would be treated in strict confidence, but once they had paid him the reward he didn't give a damn what Mrs. Gregg said or thought of him.

He finished the whisky. He was now recklessly confident.

Do it now!

Unsteadily he got to his feet and picked up the telephone receiver. A sticker on the telephone told him the number of police headquarters. He lifted the receiver. Although, by now, he was drunk, he was aware that there was no dialling tone. Muttering to himself, he replaced the receiver. He jiggled the cross-bar. The telephone remained dead. From time to time, the telephone did go dead. When, on Mrs. Gregg's instructions, he had complained, he was told by some pert girl that the exchange was over-loaded, but if he waited, the receiver would be restored.

After hesitating, he poured himself another scotch. He looked at his watch. The time was 10.38. He had plenty of time. From force of habit, he thought of what he would give Mrs. Gregg for lunch. Why bother? he thought. In a few days he would be worth two hundred thousand dollars, and he could tell the old woman to get stuffed.

He laughed, finished the scotch and let the empty glass drop on the floor.

No, he told himself. She loved her food. He would be loyal to her to the last moment. He would prepare something special for her. He searched his dazed mind. She liked chicken's breasts, smeared with mustard and grilled. He would give her that.

He reached for the telephone receiver, then he saw the cut cable. A cold shock ran through him as he stared at the dangling cable. Through the haze of scotch, cold panic swept over him.

Getting to his feet, he lurched to the door, twisted the handle and found himself locked in.

*   *   *

Amelia sat in a fat heap, her mind darting in terror. Karen Sternwood! Amelia had often been to the Sternwood's residence with her husband, attending important dinners. She had often seen Karen at these functions. Why, in the name of

157

God, she thought in despair, had Crispin, in his madness, picked this girl as a victim? If the truth came out, she would be completely finished. Sternwood would be ruthless. He would drive her out of Paradise City! This two hundred thousand dollar reward! She now felt certain that Reynolds, in his drunken state, would betray her., She heard the door open. Looking up, she saw her son, framed in the doorway.

"You are looking pensive, mother," he said, came into the room and shut the door.

She shuddered at the sight of him, her fat little hands closing into flabby fists.

He sat in a chair, fingering the Suleiman pendant.

"I am sure you have the same problem on your mind as I have. You will have to do without Reynolds. I am sorry for you, as I know you rely on him. We can no longer trust him. This reward will be too much of a temptation."

Amelia tried to speak, but the words wouldn't come.

"Don't look so distressed, mother," Crispin said. "Leave it to me. It is unfortunate, but necessary for us both."

Gasping, Amelia forced herself to say, "Crispin! What do you mean?"

Crispin smiled at her.

"I intend to dispose of Reynolds. After all, why not? He is old, an alcoholic, and no one except you, will miss him."

Amelia stared at her son in horror.

"Dispose? What are you saying?"

"Come, mother, please don't be stupid!" A sudden grating note came into Crispin's voice that made Amelia cringe. "You know what I mean . . . dispose."

Amelia leaned forward, clasping her hands and looking imploringly at her son.

"Crispin, my son," she said, he voice trembling, "please listen to your mother who loves you. You must know you are ill. I beg of you to consult someone. Dr. Raison can help you. I know he can! Please do confide in him."

Crispin smiled an evil smile.

"Is that old fool still alive? He put Uncle Martin away.

158

What would happen to you if I were put away? Have you thought of that? Would you want it known that your son, like your uncle, was locked in a padded cell? How many of your friends would you have left?" He watched her as she hid her face in her hands. "Leave this to me. There is nothing to worry about. I will find a replacement for Reynolds. After a few days, your life will continue as before." He stared at her, his eyes lighting up. "Say nothing . . . do you understand?"

At this moment, the telephone bell rang. Frowning, Crispin picked up the receiver.

"Mr. Gregg?"

"Who is it?"

"Claude Kendrick of the Kendrick Gallery."

A surge of excitment ran through Crispin.

"You have news for me? You have sold my painting?"

"It is about your painting, Mr. Gregg." Kendrick's voice was hushed. "I have had a police officer here. He wanted to know who had painted your landscape."

Crispin stiffened.

"The police? Why should they be interested in my landscape?"

"It is most extraordinary, Mr. Gregg," Kendrick said. "The police appear to think your painting is connected with these dreadful murders: this maniac killer. I can't imagine why they think so, but they do. I have told them I don't know the name of the artist, but they are pressing me. They will be here again tomorrow. Mr. Gregg! Do you have any objection to my telling them that you are the artist?"

Crispin's face turned into a savage, snarling mask.

"You tell the police nothing about me!" he snarled. "When you took my painting, you agreed I was to remain anonymous. I hold you to that! If you say anything to the police about me, Kendrick, I will put you out of business!" He slammed down the receiver.

Listening, Amelia closed her eyes and shuddered.

Now, the police!

eight

THE OFFER of a two hundred thousand dollar reward brought bedlam to the Paradise City headquarters. The telephone switchboard was jammed. A long queue of people waiting impatiently to be interviewed. Every available detective was pressed into service.

While Lepski toiled at his desk, he kept thinking of Carroll, on her birthday, disappointed he couldn't be with her. He was thankful he had given her her present before the avalanche had descended.

Ninety per cent of the eager-beavers had little or no information of use. They all claimed to have seen a tall, blond man, wearing Gucci shoes and in blue, but who was he, where he was they had no idea. They had seen him, they insisted, walking down the various city streets. Several more ambitious citizens whispered that their neighbour was tall and blond and suspicious looking. Names were taken, but as the day wore on, the detectives realized no valuable information was forth-coming. One piece of information that proved useful was supplied by a young, fat man who said he had seen Karen on Saturday evening, trying to thumb a ride.

"I know it was her," he told Jacoby. "It was around seventeen fifteen. I would have given her a ride, but she looked through me. I guess she didn't dig a fat guy like me."

At least this told Terrell who was at his desk, reading the reports as they came in, that Karen had found a driver to her taste and had hitched a ride. She had inadvertently picked on the maniac killer. This gave Terrell food for thought.

160

Around 18.00, the telephone calls dwindled and the callers faded away.

Faced with a mass of paper work that would last through the night, the detectives relaxed. None of them had had lunch. They had been sustained by coffee and cigarettes and doughnuts, produced by Charlie Tanner.

Terrell came into the Detectives' room.

"Okay, fellas," he said. "Two at the time. Go get something to eat, but be back sharp. Tom, you and Max, go first."

In a greasy spoon restaurant, a few yards from headquarters, Lepski ordered corn beef hash while Jacoby opted for a beef-burger with onions.

"Nowhere!" Lepski said in disgust. "Nothing! I had promised Carroll a celebration dinner. Who the hell would be a cop?"

"Tom," Jacoby said, "I've been thinking. Look, we have been chasing four blue jackets with golf ball buttons. We found found three of the owners with alibis. So we are chasing the fourth . . . right?"

"That doesn't need a fat lot of thought," Lepski mumbled, through a mouthful of corn beef. "Jesus! This muck isn't fit to feed a dog!"

"The fourth jacket was owned by Cyrus Gregg," Jacoby went on. "His wife says it was given to the Salvation Army who know nothing about it. Here's my thought: suppose Mrs. Gregg is lying?"

With his fork loaded with corn beef, Lepski gaped at him.

"Why should she lie for God's sake?"

"Here's something I didn't put in my report, now I keep wondering. When I talked to Levine, checking on what happened to Gregg's clothing, he had no useful information, but he did yak about the Gregg family. Right then, I was only interested in the jacket, but I've been thinking about what he said, and I think I've missed out."

Lepski chewed meat that was mainly gristle.

"So what about the family?"

161

"There's a son. According to Levine, Mrs. Gregg transferred her affection to the son, and old man Gregg was left in the wilderness. I asked what the son did, but Levine didn't know nor has he ever seen him." Jacoby paused, looking at Lepski. "As far as I know, we don't know anything about him either."

"Make your point, Max," Lepski said, laying down his knife and fork and sitting forward. "You have just said Mrs. Gregg could be lying."

"Suppose her son is the killer? Suppose he wore his father's jacket when he killed Janie Bandler? Wouldn't his mother cover up for him?"

Lepski lit a cigarette while he thought.

"You could have something, Max," he said finally. "This could certainly take care of the missing jacket. Yeah. If the description we now have fits Gregg's son, we certainly have something."

"The trouble here is Mrs. Gregg," Jacoby pointed out. "She has the ear of the mayor."

Lepski thought some more, then got to his feet.

"Say nothing to nobody, Max. I'll handle this."

Jacoby sighed.

"I was thinking maybe I could get the reward, Tom."

Lepski gaped at him.

"You? Get the reward? You tell me whenever any cop got any reward."

"Just a thought." Jacoby shrugged. "What do we do? Tell the Chief?"

"Not yet. I'll do something. Come on, let's get back."

As they left the restaurant, Lepski patted Jacoby on his broad back.

"One of these days, Max, you're going to make a great cop—like me." Then seeing a telephone booth, he went on, "Hold it! I better have a word with Carroll. Boy! Is she going to be sore!"

Jacoby waited patiently. Finally, Lepski came out of the booth, beaming.

162

"You know something, Max? She took it like a soldier. No problems. She's going to wait. How many wives would do that?"

"Don't ask me," Jacoby said. "I'm not married."

*　　　　*　　　　*

When Crispin had left her, Amelia sat, staring blankly at the opposite wall. While she stared, she wrestled with her conscience. She knew she should telephone the police and tell them that her son was a homicidal maniac and he was planning yet another murder. But she couldn't bring herself to do this.

After all, she tried to convince herself, Reynolds was old and a hopeless drunk. With him out of the way, Crispin might just settle down and these dreadful murders might cease. Sometime tonight, Crispin would dispose of Reynolds. She refused to let her mind dwell on how Crispin would get rid of the body. What was this telephone call Crispin had received from this man, Kendrick. The police?

Amelia got unsteadily to her feet. She couldn't stay a moment longer in the house! She would go to the Spanish Bay hotel. They were always kind to her. She would stay there until this dreadful affair was concluded.

She walked heavily to her bedroom. This was the moment when she missed Reynolds who always packed for her. She took a suitcase from the closet and packed what she thought she would need. As she was closing the lid of the suitcase, Crispin appeared in the doorway.

"Very wise, mother," he said, smiling at her. "Where will you stay?"

"The Spanish Bay hotel," Amelia said in a stifled voice. Crispin nodded.

"There is nothing to worry about. I will telephone you when you can return."

"I couldn't but help to overhear," Amelia said, breathing heavily. "This man, Kendrick. Why was there talk about the police?"

"Come along, mother!" There was a sudden snap in Crispin's voice. "I will carry your suitcase. Use the Rolls. I won't need it for a while."

"Crispin!" Amelia made a last feeble effort. "My son! Please. . . ."

Crispin's eyes lit up, and once again he looked like her Uncle Martin.

"Come along!" he snarled. "I want you out of here! And remember . . . say nothing!"

Defeated and frightened, Amelia followed him out of the house. Crispin put her suitcase in the trunk of the Rolls, then as she settled her bulk behind the driving wheel, he leaned forward and stared at her.

"I will telephone you in a day or so. I must arrange for someone to take care of you. Say nothing! There is nothing to worry about."

Shaking, her hands trembling, Amelia somehow started the engine. Her last thought, as she drove away, was of Reynolds.

*　　　　*　　　　*

Kendrick paced the big living room of his apartment while Louis, in a furious temper, sat on the edge of a chair, glaring at him. Kendrick had spoilt Louis's Sunday: such a lovely boy and so willing. He hadn't dared leave the boy in his apartment. The very young were so unreliable, and Louis had many choice possessions that could have tempted the boy. He had bundled him out, protesting, so he could rush over to Kendrick.

"I thought it wise, so I telephoned Mr. Gregg to explain the position," Kendrick said. "He turned exceedingly unpleasant. He says if I mention his name to the police, he would close down the gallery. He sounded vicious enough to do just that. He has money to buy me out."

"Why should he do that unless he has something to hide?" Louis demanded.

"Perhaps he does have something to hide. I don't know. I don't want to know. When Lepski comes tomorrow, cheri, we tell him nothing."

"There's a two hundred thousand dollar reward!" Louis screamed. "I heard it on the radio before I left. Do you call that nothing?"

Kendrick stared at Louis, his little eyes turning to stone.

"Listen, fool!" he said, a rasp in his voice. "Once a police informer, always a police informer. I promised Gregg not to say he was the painter of this abortion of his. If I tell the police, the word will leak. No one, in the future, will touch us!"

"So you are going to lie to Lepski!" Louis shrilled. "That will make you an accessory to murder! You are out of your mind!"

"We don't know Gregg has anything to do wth these murders!" Kendrick shouted. "Lepski says Gregg's painting is connected with these murders, but he doesn't say why. Suppose we told Lepski that Gregg did the painting and the police interrogate Gregg. He will know we have informed! Then suppose the police can prove nothing against Gregg? Then we have Gregg ruining us and the word will leak we have informed. Use your brains, cheri! We say nothing."

Louis jumped to his feet.

"I will not be involved in this!" he cried, stamping his foot. "You have spoilt my day! *You* lie to Lepski! I will not have anything to do with it!"

"Louis." Kendrick's voice turned quiet. "You are forgetting yourself. Once an informer, always an informer. Have you forgotten Kenny? How old was he . . . seven? The police are still hunting for his ravisher, Louis. Kenny could pick this man from a line-up. Once an informer, always an informer."

Blood drained out of Louis's face.

"Behave yourself, cheri," Kendrick said and smiled. "No more hysterics. If necessary you will lie to Lepski." He took off his wig and handed it to Louis. "Comb it, cheri."

With a shaking hand, Louis took out his pocket comb.

*　　　　　*　　　　　*

Ken Brandon found Mary Goodall, his previous head office secretary, waiting outside the Secomb office of the Paradise Assurance Corporation. To say he was pleased to see her would be an under-statement. Middle aged, plump and utterly efficient, Mary Goodall, to him in his present mood, was a gift from the gods.

They greeted each other, then Ken unlocked the office door, and they entered.

"How is Judge Lacey?" Mary asked as she surveyed the outer office.

"It's miraculous. We really thought he was gone, but he has made a remarkable recovery. The doctor says, with care, he could last sometime yet."

"I'm so glad. And Betty?"

"She came back with me last night. Her sister is staying with Mrs. Lacey." He saw Mary's expression as she looked around the office. "I'm afraid this dump isn't what you are used to, Mary, but I can't tell you how glad I am to have you here."

"Mr. Sternwood's secretary phoned me yesterday, telling me to take over." Mary grimaced, then smiled. "It's not quite as bad as I had imagined." Then her smile faded as she went on, "What a terrible thing to have happened! Poor Mr. Sternwood! He was so proud of his daughter!"

Ken flinched, then he walked to Karen's desk and looked at the letters and papers she had left.

"They must find this dreadful maniac," Mary went on. "This enormous reward Mr. Sternwood is offering. Two hundred thousand dollars! Surely someone will come forward."

Ken couldn't bear to think of Karen and her dreadful end.

"I hope so," he muttered, picked up the letters and papers and moved to his office. "I'll deal with these, Mary. Suppose you go through the files and get the photo of what we have been doing." Leaving her, he went into his office, closed the door and sat at his desk.

What a nightmare Sunday had been! He had read in the paper that Lu Boone had been murdered. Shocked, yet relieved that there would now be no blackmail threat, he had, later, turned on the radio. He then heard of Karen's murder. This news shattered him, and he was scarcely civil to his sister-in-law who had said, "She asked for it, living in a hippy cabin. I wouldn't be surprised if she was no better than a whore." He had telephoned Jefferson Sternwood who was unavailable. Sternwood's secretary thanked him for his call and said she hoped he would be at the Secomb office on Monday, adding that Mary Goodall was to replace Karen.

Now that Judge Lacey was out of danger, Ken couldn't wait to get home. Betty had been contacted by Dr. Heintz who asked impatiently when he could expect her. They decided to leave on the afternoon plane.

As they sat side by side in the plane, the mystery of the missing golf ball button was solved. Betty looking in her bag for a cigarette, gave a little laugh and produced the button.

"Look, darling. I carry this around as my talisman." She put her hand on his. "It's something that belongs to you."

Ken, remembering his panic, remembering how Karen had got him another button, remembering how drunk he had been, and remembering he had taken Karen into Betty's and his bed, had trouble in forcing a smile.

Now, sitting at his desk, he thought back on that Sunday. Karen was dead. Lu Boone was dead. This disloyal, disgraceful episode in his married life was now behind him. Clenching his fists, he swore to himself that it would never happen again.

On the other side of the City, Lepski parked his car within a few yards of Kendrick's gallery. He walked in to be met by Louis de Marney, pale, but with a false smile of welcome.

"Mr. Lepski! How nice! Mr. Kendrick is expecting you." He led Lepski into Kendrick's reception room.

167

Kendrick, beaming like an amiable dolphin, rose from behind his desk and offered a fat hand, but Lepski was in no mood for this kind of greeting.

Ignoring the offered hand, he said in his cop voice, "What have you got for me?"

"Please sit down, Mr. Lepski. Let us conduct this conversation in a civilized manner," Kendrick said, losing his smile. He sat down.

After hesitating, Lepski took the visitor's chair, facing Kendrick.

"Mr. Lepski, please understand that I have to protect my clients. You are asking for the name of the artist who painted this picture. That, of course, is a fair question from the police, but this artist made me promise not to reveal his name. Many artists ask me for anonymity. This may seem strange to you, but I assure you it often happens."

Lepski glared at him.

"So you know who he is?"

Kendrick took off his wig, stared at the inside of it as if he expected to find in it an ant's nest, then he replaced it, askew.

"Yes, Mr. Lepski. I know the name of the artist." He leaned forward, his little eyes like stones. "If you will explain to me why you think this artist has something to do with these murders, and if you can convince me that you have definite evidence against this artist, then, of course, I will reveal his name."

Lepski shifted in his chair. How the hell could he tell this fat queer about this rum-dum Mehitabel? How could he even tell Terrell about her? A red moon! A black sea! An orange sky!

Seeing Lepski hesitate, Kendrick moved into the offensive.

"Perhaps, Mr. Lepski, it would be better if Chief Terrell talked to me. I have always found him understanding." The dolphin smile was back. "Suppose, if I may suggest, you speak to your Chief, then he could, if he feels it necessary, speak to me."

Realizing he was defeated, Lepski got to his feet.

"Okay, Kendrick," he snarled. "So you don't give us information. I'll remember this. When you are in trouble, you'll be in real trouble," and he stormed out of the gallery.

Kendrick took off his wig and threw it up to the ceiling.

As Louis, who had been listening, came in, Kendrick beamed at him.

"You see, cheri, this stupid cop was bluffing!"

*　　　　　*　　　　　*

By 10.30, Ken Brandon had cleared his desk, had talked over the telephone to his sales director, and now decided, he would go on a hunt for new business.

As he was pushing back his chair, Mary Goodall came in.

"There's a detective wanting to speak to you, Ken. Detective Lepski."

"Send him in, Mary," Ken said, his heart beginning to race.

Lepski came in, wearing a wide, friendly grin that didn't reach his hard cop eyes.

"Hi there, Mr. Brandon!" he said. "I've brought your jacket back."

Ken gulped, forced a smile as he said, "Thank you. I hope no further trouble."

Lepski put the jacket on Ken's desk.

"The spare buttons are in the pocket, Mr. Brandon."

"Thank you."

"No problem now," Lepski went on. "I'm sorry to have worried you."

"Well, you have a job to do," Ken said.

"Yeah. This news about Miss Sternwood must have been a shock."

"Yes. Is that all, Mr. Lepski? I've just got back and I have a work load."

"I'm hoping you can help me," Lepski said. "This won't take long. Does the name Cyrus Gregg mean anything to you?"

Ken stared at him.

"Of course. He was one of my clients. He died some months ago."

"You handled his insurance?"

"That's right."

"Did Mrs. Gregg continue the coverage?"

"Yes. The policy has an automatic renewal."

"There's a son. What do you know about him, Mr. Brandon?"

"I have had no dealings with him." Ken moved impatiently. "What is this all about?"

"Have you ever seen him?"

"No."

"Know anything about him?"

"I know nothing about him. I've never seen him. So what is this all about?"

Lepski sat astride one of the upright chairs.

"I'll explain. Sit down for a moment, Mr. Brandon. This is important."

Bewildered, Ken sat behind his desk.

"We found a golf ball button right by where Janie Bandler was murdered," Lepski said. "We found that there were only four jackets with these special buttons sold in the City. We have checked out three of the jackets, including yours, and we know that you and the other two owners of the jacket have had nothing to do with Janie's murder. We were told by Mrs. Gregg that the fourth jacket, together with Mr. Gregg's other clothes, was given to the Salvation Army. We have been trying to trace this jacket, but no one at the Salvation Army has handled it. We are now wondering if Mrs. Gregg lied to us. We are wondering if her mysterious son kept his father's jacket and wore it on the night of Janie's murder. We have a description of a man, seen wearing the jacket on the day Janie was murdered. He has been described as tall, blond and wearing Gucci shoes. We have further information that this man could be an artist, painting way-out landscapes. This man is responsible not only for Janie's murder, but for Lu

Boone's and Miss Sternwood's murders. You with me so far?"

Ken eased himself back in his chair.

"I hear you," he said, "but what has all this to do with me?"

"All this I'm telling you is surmise. We don't know for sure that Gregg's son is the man we want. Mrs. Gregg draws a lot of water in this City. She has the ear of the Mayor. We want definite evidence that her son is an artist, is tall and blond and wears Gucci shoes. If we get those facts, we can interrogate him, but not before."

"I would have thought the simplest thing is for you to go to Mrs. Gregg's place and ask to speak to her son," Ken said. "What's the matter with that?"

"If it was that simple, I wouldn't be taking up your time," Lepski said. "But it isn't. Mrs. Gregg is tricky. Suppose her son has nothing to do with the murders? Suppose she refuses to let us see him, asking why we want to see him? We have no real proof so we could be in a bind. Now, Mr. Brandon, here's what I'm asking you to do. Will you go to the Gregg's place and ask to see the son? Say you understand he has valuable paintings and he might like to insure them. We must know he is an artist and he matches up with this description we have: tall, blond, and possibly, wearing Gucci shoes."

Ken shook his head.

"I don't want anything to do with it," he said firmly. "This is police business. Don't tell me you can't call and see Gregg yourself. Why drag me into this?"

Lepski shifted in his chair.

"Let me spell this out, Mr. Brandon. We could be making a mistake. Gregg may not be the killer we are after. The Gregg family employ the smartest and toughest attorney in this City. If we are wrong about Gregg, we could get landed with a libel action. All I am asking you to do is to take a look at Gregg. If he doesn't match up with the description we have of this killer, that's it. Maybe, you can sell him some insurance. If he does match up, then we move in and arrest him."

Again Ken shook his head.

"I won't have anything to do with this."

With his wolf's smile, Lepski played his trump card.

"You are forgetting one important thing, Mr. Brandon. If Gregg is the man we are after, and you identify him for us, you will pick up the reward Mr. Sternwood is offering . . . two hundred thousand dollars."

Ken gaped.

"Two hundred thousand dollars? Me? You must be kidding!"

"No kid, Mr. Brandon. I assure you if you identify Gregg as the man we want, you get the reward."

Two hundred thousand dollars!

Ken felt a surge of excitement run through him. What couldn't he do with money like that! Into his mind swam a picture of a new house in a better district, a big swimming pool, better cars for Betty and himself! Betty could even give up working for Dr. Heintz! He could even give up his job and start his own business!

Watching him, Lepski saw Ken was hooked.

"If you really mean I'll get the reward if I identify Gregg," Ken said, "then I'll co-operate."

Lepski beamed at him.

"Providing your evidence leads to Gregg's arrest and conviction," he said, "then you get the reward. I guarantee that."

Ken drew in a deep breath.

"Okay." His mind was churning with the thought of owning two hundred thousand dollars. "So what do you want me to do?"

Lepski knew that Brandon could be dealing with a dangerous killer, but he held back this information, fearing Brandon might chicken out if he realized he could be walking into trouble. Brandon must be protected, Lepski told himself.

"I'll set it up," he said, and picking up the telephone receiver, he dialled police headquarters. He asked for Max Jacoby. After a delay, Jacoby came on the line.

"Max . . . Tom," Lepski said. "That idea you had could jell. I want you to come fast to Paradise City Assurance, Secomb. We have a trip to make."

"I'm up to my eyes in work!" Jacoby protested.

"Who the hell cares? Get moving, and fast!" Lepski hung up. Then smiling at Ken, he said, "No problem. In half an hour, we'll get going. Here's what you have to do."

His mind only half concentrating, as he kept thinking what he would do with two hundred thousand dollars, Ken listened.

*   *   *

Lepski, driving his car with Max Jacoby at his side, followed Ken's car as he headed for Acacia Drive.

Jacoby was worried.

"I hope to God you know what you are doing," he said, as Lepski slowed the car in a traffic block. "We are sticking our necks out! The Chief will have our hides if something goes wrong. You should have reported to him first!"

"Relax," Lepski said. "You know as well as I do, if I told the Chief what's cooking, he would have put his foot on it. Between the two of us, Max, we could bust this case."

"How about Brandon?" Jacoby demanded. "Suppose he walks into trouble? Suppose Gregg is our man? We know the killer is a psychopath. Suppose he kills Brandon? What will happen to us?"

"Take it easy, Max," Lepski said, not feeling all that easy himself. "We are giving Brandon protection, aren't we? That's why I have you with me."

"Did you warn Brandon that he could be walking into trouble?"

"Look, Max, Brandon wants the reward. He is willing to co-operate," Lepski said, knowing he should have warned Brandon. "If he fingers Gregg for us, he picks up two hundred grand."

"Not if he is killed!" Jacoby snapped. "And is this such a

hot idea of yours to get him to wear the golf ball jacket?"

"If Gregg is our man, the sight of that jacket could throw him," Lepski said. "If he isn't our man, then the jacket will mean nothing to him. These psychos crack easily under pressure. Anyway, no one picks up two hundred thousand dollars for nothing."

"Did you warn Brandon he could be walking into trouble?" Jacoby persisted.

Lepski shifted in his driving seat.

"I told him not to go into the villa. I told him to stay right on the doorstep so we could watch him all the time. Just relax for the love of Pete!"

By now they had reached Acacia Drive, and as arranged, Ken drew up within a hundred yards of the Gregg villa.

"Let's go," Lepski said, sliding out of the car. Followed by Jacoby, he walked to Ken's car.

"Go ahead, Mr. Brandon," he said, looking through the open car window. "Just remember, don't go into the villa. Tell the butler you want a quick word with Mr. Gregg. If he invites you in, tell him you're badly parked and it won't take a minute. All you have to do is take a long look at Gregg. Okay?"

Ken began to read the message. His hands, resting on the steering wheel, turned clammy.

"Gregg could be dangerous?" There was a sudden quaver in his voice.

Lepski shifted impatiently.

"Take it easy," he said. "There's a butler. Maybe Mrs. Gregg is there. You have nothing to worry about. You stay right on the doorstep where we can see you, and there's no problem.

Ken began to sweat.

"But suppose I have to go inside?"

"You don't!" Lepski barked in his cop voice. "If Gregg is our man, he won't start anything with the butler and his mother around. You could be picking up two hundred thousand bucks!" Reaching through the open car window, he

174

patted Ken on his shoulder. "You have no problems, Mr. Brandon. We are right behind you."

Ken hesitated, then he thought again of the reward. He forced an uneasy smile.

"Okay. . . . I'm on my way."

He drove to the entrance of the Gregg villa, looking in his driving mirror to make sure Lepski and Jacoby were following him on foot. He was self conscious about wearing the golf ball jacket, but Lepski had insisted he should wear it. Then parking outside the villa, he left the car and walked slowly up the drive. He glanced back, and was in time to see the two detectives had entered and were ducking out of sight into a vast clump of flowering shrubs.

He walked up to the front door of the villa, then, bracing himself, he thumbed the bell. He heard the chimes of bells somewhere inside the villa. He waited, feeling the hot sun on his back, his heart thumping. Nothing happened. He looked uneasily behind him, but there were no signs of the two detectives. He felt frighteningly alone. He thumbed the bell again. Apart from the sound of the bells, a heavy silence brooded over the villa.

He took out his handkerchief and mopped his sweating face. He began to relax. Maybe, he told himself, no one was home. He felt a disappointed let-down. The dream of two hundred thousand dollars began to fade.

After waiting another long moment, he took a step back. Then almost relieved, he turned to walk back to his car. At this moment, the front door of the villa opened.

Watching, Lepski and Jacoby, concealed behind flowering shrubs, saw Ken start down the steps, pause and turn around. They saw the front door open, but that was all they could see. Ken, moving back to the top step, blotted out their view. All they could see was his broad back.

The first thing Ken saw was a pair of highly polished black Gucci shoes. Then looking up, he found himself confronted by a tall, blond man who was smiling at him.

Tall! Blond! Gucci shoes! This was the man the police

175

were searching for! Ken's mouth turned dry. His instincts screamed to him to turn and run, but he remained motionless, like a rabbit hypnotized by a stoat.

"Yes?" Crispin said, his voice gentle.

Ken pulled himself together.

"Excuse me for disturbing you," he said. "Are you Mr. Gregg?"

"That's a nice jacket you are wearing," Crispin said. "My father had one just like that. What did you want?"

Ken licked his dry lips.

"I am sure I am disturbing you. Some other time. I won't bother you now."

He took a step back, then paused as he found himself looking at an automatic pistol Crispin was pointing at him.

"Do exactly what I tell you," Crispin said, an edge to his voice. "If you don't want to be shot, come in."

Although Ken had often read in newspapers and in detective stories of people held at gun point, it wasn't until this moment, he understood the terror of a pointing gun.

Crispin moved back into the lobby.

"Come in," he repeated.

Ken thought of the two detectives, hidden and watching. Lepski had told him not to enter the villa, but the threatening gun gave him no alternative. Moving with leaden feet, he crossed the threshold and walked into the lobby.

"Very wise of you," Crispin said. "Now shut the door."

His heart pounding, Ken paused and looked down the drive, but saw nothing of the two detectives. He closed the door.

"Now shoot the bolts," Crispin said.

Ken found two heavy bolts: one at the top of the door, the other at the bottom. His hand shaking, he did as he was told.

"Now go upstairs," Crispin said.

Supporting his shaking legs by holding onto the banister rail, Ken mounted the stairs. Crispin followed him.

"To your right," Crispin said. "Go in."

Ken entered Crispin's luxurious living room.

"Sit down." The gun pointed to a chair, away from the picture window.

Ken sat down, resting his sweating hands on his knees.

Crispin perched himself on the edge of the big desk.

"You must excuse the gun," he said. "I am nervous of being kidnapped. I always take precautions. Who are you?"

Maybe, Ken thought, this is going to work out all right. He could understand a man of Gregg's worth being nervous about being kidnapped.

"My name is Brandon," he said, trying to steady his voice. "I represent the Paradise City Assurance. I've called to see if you would be interested in insuring your paintings. I assure you, Mr. Gregg, I am quite harmless."

Crispin stared at him for a long moment.

"Insure my paintings? How do you know I paint? Did Kendrick tell you?"

Again Ken felt a sick feeling of fear. Lepski had asked him to verify that Gregg was a painter. The fact that he was now saying he was, plus the description Lepski had given, told Ken this tall, blond man who was staring at him was without any doubt the lunatic killer who had so horribly murdered Karen Sternwood. He felt the blood drain out of his face.

Watching him, Crispin asked again, "Did Kendrick tell you?"

Ken had had business dealings with Kendrick, insuring some of Kendrick's treasures.

"In confidence, Mr. Gregg," he said, his voice husky, "Mr. Kendrick did mention you had valuable paintings."

"Yes, they are valuable." Crispin dropped the gun into his pocket. "Again, I apologize for scaring you, Mr. Brandon, but in these days, unknown callers can be dangerous."

"Of course." Ken again began to relax. "Would it interest you, Mr. Gregg for us to cover your paintings?"

"Would they have to be valued?"

"Not necessarily. You tell us what you think they are worth, and we will quote."

"Perhaps you would care to see some of my work, Mr.

Brandon?" Crispin said and stood up.

"I am no judge," Ken said and got to his feet. "I won't waste your time further, Mr. Gregg." His one thought now was to escape from the villa. "Just tell me approximately what you want us to cover your work for, and I will write to you, quoting premiums." He started moving towards the door.

"It won't take a moment," Crispin said. "I am working on a particularly interesting study. I must show it to you." As he stared at Ken, he fingered the Suleiman pendant, and he smiled.

"I have another appointment," Ken said desperately. "Some other time, Mr. Gregg. Suppose I call and see you tomorrow? You can tell me the value of your paintings and I can quote you."

As Ken opened the door, Crispin his opal coloured eyes suddenly alight, moved towards him.

*   *   *

Crouching behind the flowering shrubs, Lepski, with Jacoby by his side, watched Ken move forward and enter the villa.

"The stupid jerk!" Lepski exploded. "He's gone in! I told him to stay outside! You heard me, didn't you?"

"I heard what you told him," Jacoby said, showing alarm. "So what are we going to do?"

Lepski wiped his sweating face with the back of his hand.

"The stupid pea-brain! I told him whatever he did, he was to stay on the door-step, and not to go in!"

Staring at the villa, the two detectives saw the front door close.

"So what are we going to do?" Jacoby said.

"What can we do? Could be Mrs. Gregg opened the door and Brandon felt he had to go in." Lepski shoved his hat to the back of his head in exasperation.

"If Mrs. Gregg didn't open the door: if the butler didn't open the door but Gregg did, we'd better do something," Jacoby said. "Tom! I get the feeling this caper has turned sour."

"Just suppose Gregg isn't our man," Lepski said feverishly. "Just suppose Brandon walks out in the next few minutes. If we go charging in there, we could start a stink that could put us back on the beat."

"But suppose Gregg is our man?" Jacoby said. "Suppose Gregg kills him? We'd better do something."

"Yeah." Lepski straightened. "I'll handle this, Max. You stay right here". He took out his .38 police special. "If there's trouble, I'll fire a shot, and you come running. Okay?"

"What's your idea?"

"I'll say I'm checking on this goddam golf ball jacket again," Lepski said, then leaving Jacoby, he walked swiftly across the lawn and to the front entrance of the villa. He returned his gun to its holster and leaving his jacket open so he could grab his gun, he thumbed the door bell.

As Crispin moved towards Ken, his eyes glittering, the bell of the telephone standing on his desk began ringing.

The sound brought Crispin to an abrupt halt. He pointed to a chair away from the door.

"Sit down a moment, Mr. Brandon." The edge to his voice and his expression was such that Ken, now thoroughly frightened, hurriedly sat down.

Not turning his back to Ken, Crispin moved to the desk and lifted the receiver.

"Yes? Who is it?"

"Sergeant Beigler. City police. Is that Mr. Gregg?" Watching, Ken saw Crispin's face turn into a snarling mask.

"Yes. What is it?"

"You are wanted at the Paradise hospital, Mr. Gregg. I'm sorry to tell you there has been an accident."

"My mother?"

"Yes, sir. Apparently she lost control of her car and hit a truck."

"Is she badly hurt?" Crispin asked eagerly.

"I regret to tell you, sir, she died on arrival."

A smile that sent a chill through Ken, played around

Crispin's lips.

"Thank you," he said. "Please notify Mr. Lewishon, my attorney. He will attend to the necessary formalities," and he hung up. He turned and grinned gleefully at Ken. "I have just had excellent news, Mr. Brandon. My mother has been killed in a road accident. At last, I am free of her!"

Regarding him with horror, Ken got to his feet.

"I must go, Mr. Gregg."

"But first you must see my art." Crispin stared at Ken. "You knew Miss Karen Sternwood?"

Ken gulped, then nodded.

"I am working on her portrait. It's just a rough sketch, but I want your opinion."

All Ken could think of was to get out and away from this madman.

"Please excuse me, Mr. Gregg," he said, his voice a croak. "I just have to go now."

Crispin's smile turned evil.

"I don't want to get annoyed with you, Mr. Brandon," he said, fingering the Suleiman pendant. "I assure you I can be exceedingly unpleasant with people who annoy me." He waved to a door at the end of the room. "Go ahead, please."

Regarding this man, Ken knew he was in deadly danger. He walked across the room to the door indicated, then he heard, somewhere in the villa, the sound of the front door bell. He paused and looked quickly at Crispin.

Lepski? Ken thought. God! He hoped it was!

"Now who could that be?" Crispin said, half to himself. "Never mind. Whoever it is can't get in. You bolted the door securely, didn't you, Mr. Brandon? Now come along. I want you to see my sketch of this little whore." He regarded Ken. "She was a little whore, wasn't she?"

The bell rang again.

"Do what I tell you!" Crispin snarled as he saw Ken hesitating. Shocked by the demoniacal expression on Crispin's face, Ken opened the door and walked into the studio.

Standing before the front door, Lepski, in a slight panic that no one answered the bell, looked to right and left. All the windows of the downstairs rooms were barred.

Seeing there was no answer, Jacoby came out of the shrubs and joined Lepski.

"No one's answering," Lepski said.

"Bust in the door?"

"We can't do that without a warrant," Lepski rang the bell again.

Then suddenly the door was flung open and they were confronted by a tall, coloured woman, her face contorted with terror, her big eyes rolling. She put her hand to her mouth, signing to the two gaping detectives to keep silent. Frantically, she beckoned them in. Such was her terror, both Lepski and Jacoby drew their guns as they followed her into the lobby.

With a stabbing motion, she pointed down the passage to a door at the far end, making a soft mumbling noise.

Signalling Jacoby to stay with the woman, Lepski went silently to the door and threw it open. What he saw in the room made him catch his breath.

Lying on a bed was the tattered and mutilated remains of a man Lepski scarcely recognized as the drunken butler, Reynolds. He saw Reynolds was beyond help, and his mind flashed to Brandon. Where was he?

Chrissy, moaning softly, was shaking Jacoby's arm and pointing up the stairs, then with surprising strength, she pushed Jacoby out of her way and ran from the villa.

"Upstairs," Jacoby whispered.

Lepski nodded and began to mount the stairs. Jacoby followed him. On the landing, Lepski paused. Jacoby went down on one knee, covering Lepski.

Through the door of the studio, Lepski heard Crispin say, "What do you think of it, Mr. Brandon? Have I caught her likeness?" Ken scarcely looked at the sketch of Karen Sternwood that Crispin was holding up. He was staring with horror at the painting of Lu Boone's head, at the gruesome painting of Janie Bandler and at the portrait of Mrs. Gregg.

181

Then his eyes moved to the other sick canvasses lining the walls.

"I see you are looking at my art," Crispin said, "but please concentrate. What do you think of my sketch of the little whore?"

Lepski nodded to Jacoby, then took four quick steps to the door, threw it open and shouted in his cop voice, "Stay still! Police!" His gun covered Crispin.

Ken drew in a long, deep breath. He slowly backed to the door.

"He has a gun in his pocket," he said breathlessly.

Crispin appeared to be completely relaxed. He raised his hands in a token of surrender.

"Of course, Chrissy let you in. Stupid of me to have forgotten Chrissy." He smiled. "Yes, there is a gun in my pocket. It belonged to my father."

"Max, get it!" Lepski snapped. "Stay still, Gregg."

Jacoby moved around to the back of Crispin while Lepski kept him covered. Jacoby found the gun and stepped away.

Crispin continued to smile.

"You two are badly paid detectives. You, Mr. Brandon, are a badly paid salesman," he said. "Let us make a deal. I offer two million dollars to be divided between the three of you and we will forget what has happened. What do you say?"

"Money won't buy you anything, Gregg! You have reached the end of your road," Lepski said.

"Shall we make it three million?" Crispin asked, still smiling.

Without taking his eyes off Crispin, Lepski said, "Max get homicide here and the meat wagon."

As Jacoby moved to the telephone, Crispin waved his hand to his paintings.

"What do you think of my art?" he asked Lepski and he moved forward slowly. "I suppose people not used to modern art would think I was mad, but what do you think?"

Lepski's eyes swept around the studio and what he saw not only sickened him but threw him off his guard, then he realized Crispin was very close to him.

"Stay right where you are!" he barked and lifted his gun.

"Don't be nervous of me," Crispin said, his opal coloured eyes lighting up. "I am unarmed," then still smiling, his finger pressed the ruby of the Sulliman pendant, and weaving forward, he struck as Lepski shot him.

*　　　　*　　　　*

Two days later, Max Jacoby sneaked into a private room at the Paradise Clinic where Lepski, feeling sorry for himself, lay in bewildered style.

"How are you feeling, Tom?" Jacoby asked as he came to the bed.

"What's going on?" Lepski demanded. "Why am I in this setup?"

"Sternwood insisted you should be given the VIP treatment. He's picking up the tab. You are a hero, Tom," and Jacoby grinned. "How are you feeling?"

"I'll survive," Lepski said and released a moan. "That sonofabitch nearly had me."

"Take it easy. You killed him. The press are yelling to interview you. Pete Hamilton is walking all over the ceiling to get you on T.V."

Lepski brightened.

"How about the Chief?"

"I fixed that. I told him you and I were checking on the golf ball jacket and we walked right into it. Brandon says he was trying to sell Gregg insurance when he recognized Gregg as the killer. There are no problems, Tom. Just recover. The boys plan to throw you a party as soon as you get out of here."

Lepski grinned.

"I'm going to tell the Chief he should up-grade you, Max. You are a goddam fine pal."

Jacoby beamed.

"It's already fixed. I'll be a second grade from tomorrow."

"And Brandon?"

183

"He's getting the reward."

"I guess he's earned it. He had a hairy time."

"He wants to throw a party for you too." Jacoby began to move to the door. "Carroll's waiting, Tom. I just wanted you to know you have no problems."

Two minutes later, Carroll, starry eyed, carrying a bouquet of flowers and an elaborate basket of fruit, swept in.

"Oh, Tom, darling!"

"Hi, honey!" Lepski said. "You look good enough to get into bed with me!"

"Now, don't be coarse," Carroll said. "They say you nearly died."

"So what? I didn't! Am I glad to see you!"

"Tom, you are making headlines! You'll be on television! I'm so proud of you!"

"Fine!" Lepski preened himself. "I'll be out at the end of the week, then you and I will celebrate. We'll go to the Spanish Bay grillroom and we'll have a ball."

Carroll sat by the bed and took his hand.

"We can't afford the Spanish Bay, darling. That costs the earth."

"Who cares? What's money for? We'll celebrate at the Spanish Bay . . . that's a promise!"

"Tom! I want to ask you something. It has been worrying me. Did Mehitabel Bessinger's clues help you?"

Lepski hesitated, then decided that a lie would save him another bottle of Cutty Sark.

"That old rum-dum? Forget it, honey. Her clues were as useful as a hole in the head."

"Oh, Tom! I really thought. . . ."

"Never mind about her," Lepski said. "Go and lock the door. I want to prove to you I'm not as badly hurt as I am supposed to be."

After hesitating, Carroll crossed the room and locked the door.

>>> If you've enjoyed this book and would like to discover more great vintage crime and thriller titles, as well as the most exciting crime and thriller authors writing today, visit: >>>

The Murder Room
Where Criminal Minds Meet

themurderroom.com